Edna Lyall

Derrick Vaughan, Novelist

Edna Lyall

Derrick Vaughan, Novelist

ISBN/EAN: 9783337028930

Printed in Europe, USA, Canada, Australia, Japan

Cover: Foto ©Raphael Reischuk / pixelio.de

More available books at **www.hansebooks.com**

DERRICK VAUGHAN

NOVELIST

By EDNA LYALL

AUTHOR OF "DONOVAN," "WE TWO," "IN THE GOLDEN DAYS,
"KNIGHT ERRANT," ETC.

"IT is only through deep sympathy that a man can become a great artist."—LEWES'S *Life of Goethe*.

"Sympathy is feeling related to an object, whilst sentiment is the same feeling seeking itself alone."—ARNOLD TOYNBEE.

EIGHTEENTH THOUSAND

LONDON
METHUEN AND CO.
18 BURY STREET, W.C.
1889.

Edna Lyall.

The Christian World.
13 & 14. Fleet Street.
London. E.C.

Edna Lyall's new novel,

Hope the Hermit: a Romance of Borrowdale —
will be published exclusively in the columns of
The Christian World, commencing in the issue of
January 6.   In this story the author deals
with one of her favourite periods, the 17th century.
It is a love story, and treats of the days of the
English Revolution, the accession of William & Mary, &
the Jacobite plots, with which the Queen had to con-
tend while King William was away at the war. The
scene is chiefly laid in the neighbourhood of Keswick, or
in London. Among the real characters introduced are
Archbishop. Tillotson, George Fox the Quaker, and
Lady Temple, so well known from the charming 'Love
Letters of Dorothy Osborne'. Hope the Hermit will com-
mence in The Christian World of Thursday, January 6.

TO MY DEAR FRIEND

MARY DAVIES

[CHIEF SONGSTRESS OF WALES,]

I DEDICATE THIS BOOK.

DERRICK VAUGHAN—NOVELIST

CHAPTER I.

" Nothing fills a child's mind like a large old mansion ;
better if un- or partially occupied ; peopled with the
spirits of deceased members of the county and
Justices of the Quorum. Would I were buried in
the peopled solitude of one, with my feelings at seven
years old ! "—From *Letters of* CHARLES LAMB.

To attempt a formal biography of Derrick
Vaughan would be out of the question, even
though he and I have been more or less thrown
together since we were both in the nursery.
But I have an odd sort of wish to note down
roughly just a few of my recollections of him,
and to show how his fortunes gradually de-
veloped, being perhaps stimulated to make the
attempt by certain irritating remarks which one .
overhears now often enough at clubs or in drawing-rooms, or indeed wherever one goes. "Derrick

A

Vaughan," say these authorities of the world of small-talk, with that delightful air of omniscience which invariably characterises them, " why, he simply leapt into fame.   He is one of the favour- ites of fortune.   Like Byron, he woke one morn- ing and found himself famous."

Now this sounds well enough, but it is a long way from the truth, and I—Sydney Wharncliffe, of the Inner Temple, Barrister-at-law—desire while the past few years are fresh in my mind to write a true version of my friend's career.

Every one knows his face.   Has it not appeared in " Noted Men," and—gradually de- teriorating according to the price of the paper and the quality of the engraving—in many another illustrated journal ?   Yet somehow these works of art don't satisfy me, and, as I write, I see before me something very different from the latest photograph by Messrs. Paul and Reynard.

I see a large-featured, broad-browed, English face, a trifle heavy-looking when in repose, yet a thorough, honest, manly face, with a complexion neither dark nor fair, with brown hair and moustache, and with light hazel eyes that look out on the world quietly enough. You might talk to him for long in an ordinary way and never suspect that he was a genius ; but when you have him to yourself, when some conscious-ness of sympathy rouses him, he all at once becomes a different being. His quiet eyes kindle, his face becomes full of life—you wonder that you ever thought it heavy or commonplace. Then the world interrupts in some way and, just as a hermit-crab draws down its shell with a comically rapid movement, so Derrick suddenly retires into himself.

Thus much for his outer man.

For the rest, there are of course the neat little accounts of his birth-place, his parentage, his education, &c., &c., published with the list of his works in due order, with the engravings in the illustrated papers. But these tell little of the real life of the man.

Carlyle, in one of his finest passages, says that " A true delineation of the smallest man and his scene of pilgrimage through life is capable of interesting the greatest men ; that all men are to an unspeakable degree brothers, each man's life a strange emblem of every man's ; and, that human portraits faithfully drawn are of all pictures the welcomest on human walls." And though I don't profess to give a portrait, but merely a sketch, I will endeavour to sketch faithfully, and possibly in the future my work may fall into the hands of some of those worthy people who imagine that my friend leapt into fame at a bound, or of those comfortable mortals who seem to think that a novel is turned out as easily as water from a tap.

There is, however, one thing I can never do :— I am quite unable to put into words my friend's intensely strong feeling with regard to the sacredness of his profession. It seemed to me not unlike the feeling of Isaiah when, in the vision, his mouth had been touched with the celestial fire. And I can only hope that something of this may be read between my very inadequate lines.

Looking back, I fancy Derrick must have been a clever child. But he was not precocious, and in some respects was even decidedly backward. I can see him now, it is my first clear recollection of him, leaning back in the corner of my father's carriage as we drove from the New-

market station to our summer home at Mondisfield. He and I were small boys of eight, and
Derrick had been invited for the holidays, while
his twin brother—if I remember right—indulged
in typhoid fever at Kensington. He was shy
and silent, and the ice was not broken until we
passed Silvery Steeple.

"That," said my father, "is a ruined church;
it was destroyed by Cromwell in the Civil Wars."

In an instant the small quiet boy sitting beside
me was transformed. His eyes shone; he sprang
forward and thrust his head far out of the
window, gazing at the old ivy-covered tower as
long as it remained in sight.

"Was Cromwell really once there?" he asked
with breathless interest.

"So they say," replied my father, looking with
an amused smile at the face of the questioner,
in which eagerness, delight, and reverence were
mingled. "Are you an admirer of the Lord
Protector?"

"He is my greatest hero of all," said Derrick
fervently. "Do you think—oh, do you think he
possibly can ever have come to Mondisfield?"

My father thought not, but said there was an

old tradition that the Hall had been attacked by the Royalists, and the bridge over the moat defended by the owner of the house ; but he had no great belief in the story, for which, indeed, there seemed no evidence.

Derrick's eyes during this conversation were something wonderful to see, and long after, when we were not actually playing at anything, I used often to notice the same expression stealing over him, and would cry out, " There is the man defending the bridge again, I can see him in your eyes ! Tell me what happened to him next ! "

Then, generally pacing to and fro in the apple walk, or sitting astride the bridge itself, Derrick would tell me of the adventures of my ancestor, Paul Wharncliffe, who performed incredible feats of valour, and who was to both of us a most real person. On wet days he wrote his story in a copy-book, and would have worked at it for hours had my mother allowed him, though of the manual part of the work he had, and has always retained, the greatest dislike. I remember well the comical ending of this first story of his. He skipped over an interval of ten years, represented on the page by ten laboriously made stars, and did for his hero in the following lines :—

"And now, reader, let us come into Mondisfield churchyard. There are three tombstones. On one is written, 'Mr. Paul Wharncliffe.'"

The story was no better than the productions of most eight-year-old children, the written story at least. But curiously enough it proved to be the germ of the celebrated romance " At Strife," which Derrick wrote in after years; and he himself maintains that his picture of life during the Civil War would have been much less graphic had he not lived so much in the past during his various visits to Mondisfield.

It was at his second visit, when we were nine, that I remember his announcing his intention of being an author when he was grown up. My mother still delights in telling the story. She was sitting at work in the south parlour one day, when I dashed into the room calling out:

"Derrick's head is stuck between the banisters in the gallery; come quick, mother, come quick!"

She ran up the little winding staircase, and there, sure enough, in the musician's gallery, was poor Derrick, his manuscript and pen on the floor and his head in durance vile.

"You silly boy!" said my mother, a little frightened when she found that to get the head back was no easy matter. "What made you put it through?"

"You look like King Charles at Carisbrooke," I cried, forgetting how much Derrick would resent the speech.

And being released at that moment he took me by the shoulders and gave me an angry shake or two, as he said vehemently, "I'm not like King Charles! King Charles was a liar."

I saw my mother smile a little as she separated us.

"Come, boys, don't quarrel," she said. "And Derrick will tell me the truth, for indeed I am curious to know why he thrust his head in such a place."

"I wanted to make sure," said Derrick, "whether Paul Wharncliffe could see Lady Lettice when she took the falcon on her wrist below in the passage. I mustn't say he saw her if it's impossible, you know. Authors have to be quite true in little things, and I mean to be an author."

" But," said my mother, laughing at the great
earnestness of the hazel eyes, " could not your
hero look over the top of the rail ? "

" Well, yes," said Derrick. " He would have
done that, but you see it's so dreadfully high
and I couldn't get up. But I tell you what, Mrs.
Wharncliffe, if it wouldn't be giving you a great
deal of trouble—I'm sorry you were troubled to
get my head back again—but if you would just
look over, since you are so tall, and I'll run down
and act Lady Lettice."

" Why couldn't Paul go downstairs and look
at the lady in comfort ? " asked my mother.

Derrick mused a little.

" He might look at her through a crack in the
door at the foot of the stairs, perhaps, but that
would seem mean, somehow. It would be a
pity, too, not to use the gallery ; galleries are
uncommon, you see, and you can get cracked
doors anywhere. And, you know, he was obliged to look at her when she couldn't see him,
because their fathers were on different sides in
the war, and dreadful enemies."

When school-days came, matters went on
much in the same way ; there was always an

abominably scribbled tale stowed away in Derrick's desk, and he worked infinitely harder than
I did, because there was always before him this
determination to be an author and to prepare
himself for the life. But he wrote merely from
love of it, and with no idea of publication until
the beginning of our last year at Oxford, when,
having reached the ripe age of one-and-twenty,
he determined to delay no longer, but to plunge
boldly into his first novel.

He was seldom able to get more than six or
eight hours a week for it, because he was reading rather hard, so that the novel progressed but
slowly. Finally, to my astonishment, it came to
a dead stand-still.

I have never made out exactly what was
wrong with Derrick then, though I know that
he passed through a terrible time of doubt and
despair. I spent part of the Long with him
down at Ventnor, where his mother had been
ordered for her health. She was devoted to
Derrick, and, as far as I can understand, he was
her chief comfort in life. Major Vaughan, the
husband, had been out in India for years ; the
only daughter was married to a rich manufacturer

at Birmingham, who had a constitutional dislike to mothers-in-law, and as far as possible eschewed their company ; while Lawrence, Derrick's twin brother, was for ever getting into scrapes, and was into the bargain the most unblushingly selfish fellow I ever had the pleasure of meeting.

"Sydney," said Mrs. Vaughan to me one afternoon when we were in the garden, "Derrick seems to me unlike himself, there is a division between us which I never felt before. Can you tell me what is troubling him ?"

She was not at all a good-looking woman, but she had a very sweet, wistful face, and I never looked at her sad eyes without feeling ready to go through fire and water for her. I tried now to make light of Derrick's depression.

"He is only going through what we all of us go through," I said, assuming a cheerful tone. "He has suddenly discovered that life is a great riddle, and that the things he has accepted in blind faith are, after all, not so sure."

She sighed.

"Do all go through it ?" she said thoughtfully. "And how many, I wonder, get beyond ?"

"Few enough," I replied moodily. Then, remembering my *rôle*,—" But Derrick will get through ; he has a thousand things to help him which others have not,—you, for instance. And then I fancy he has a sort of insight which most of us are without."

" Possibly," she said. " As for me, it is little that I can do for him. Perhaps you are right, and it is true that once in a life at any rate we all have to go into the wilderness alone."

That was the last summer I ever saw Derrick's mother ; she took a chill the following Christmas and died after a few days' illness. But I have always thought her death helped Derrick in a way that her life might have failed to do. For although he never, I fancy, quite recovered from the blow, and to this day cannot speak of her without tears in his eyes, yet when he came back to Oxford he seemed to have found the answer to the riddle, and though older, sadder and graver than before, had quite lost the restless dissatisfaction that for some time had clouded his life. In a few months, moreover, I noticed a fresh sign that he was out of the wood. Coming into his rooms one day I found him sitting in the cushioned window-seat, reading

over and correcting some sheets of blue foolscap.

" At it again ? " I asked.

He nodded.

" I mean to finish the first volume here. For
the rest I must be in London."

" Why ? " I asked, a little curious as to this
unknown art of novel-making.

" Because," he replied, " one must be in the
heart of things to understand how Lynwood was
affected by them."

" Lynwood ! I believe you are always thinking
of him ! " (Lynwood was the hero of his novel.)

" Well so I am nearly—so I must be, if the
book is to be any good."

" Read me what you have written," I said,
throwing myself back in a rickety but tolerably
comfortable arm-chair which Derrick had inherited with the rooms.

He hesitated a moment, being always very
diffident about his own work ; but presently,
having provided me with a cigar and made a
good deal of unnecessary work in arranging the
sheets of the manuscript, he began to read aloud,
rather nervously, the opening chapters of the

book now so well known under the title of
" Lynwood's Heritage."

I had heard nothing of his for the last four
years, and was amazed at the gigantic stride he
had made in the interval.   For, spite of a certain
crudeness, it seemed to me a most powerful story;
it rushed straight to the point with no wavering,
no beating about the bush ; it flung itself into
the problems of the day with a sort of sublime
audacity ; it took hold of one ; it whirled one
along with its own inherent force, and drew forth
both laughter and tears, for Derrick's power of
pathos had always been his strongest point.

All at once he stopped reading.

" Go on ! " I cried impatiently.

" That is all," he said, gathering the sheets together.

" You stopped in the middle of a sentence ! " I
cried in exasperation.

" Yes," he said quietly, " for six months."

" You provoking fellow ! why, I wonder ? "

" Because I didn't know the end."

" Good heavens !   And do you know it now ? "

He looked me full in the face, and there was
an expression in his eyes which puzzled me.

"I believe I do," he said ; and, getting up, he crossed the room, put the manuscript away in a drawer, and returning, sat down in the window-seat again, looking out on the narrow, paved street below, and at the grey buildings opposite.

I knew very well that he would never ask me what I thought of the story—that was not his way.

"Derrick!" I exclaimed, watching his impassive face, "I believe after all you are a genius."

I hardly know why I said "after all," but till that moment it had never struck me that Derrick was particularly gifted. He had so far got through his Oxford career creditably, but then he had worked hard ; his talents were not of a showy order. I had never expected that he would set the Thames on fire. Even now it seemed to me that he was too dreamy, too quiet, too devoid of the pushing faculty to succeed in the world.

My remark made him laugh incredulously.

"Define a genius," he said.

For answer I pulled down his beloved Imperial Dictionary and read him the following quotation from De Quincey: "Genius is that mode of intellectual power which moves in alliance with the genial nature; *i.e.,* with the capacities of pleasure and pain ; whereas talent has no vestige of such an alliance, and is perfectly independent of all human sensibilities."

"Let me think ! You can certainly enjoy things a hundred times more than I can—and as for suffering, why you were always a great hand at that. Now listen to the great Dr. Johnson and see if the cap fits. 'The true genius is a mind of large general powers accidentally determined in some particular direction.'"

"'Large general powers'!—yes, I believe after all you have them with—alas, poor Derrick ! one notable exception—the mathematical faculty. You were always bad at figures. We will stick to De Quincey's definition, and for heaven's sake, my dear fellow, do get Lynwood out of that awful plight ! No wonder you were depressed when you lived all this age with such a sentence unfinished ! "

"For the matter of that," said Derrick, "he can't get out till the end of the book ; but I can begin to go on with him now."

" And when you leave Oxford ? "

" Then I mean to settle down in London—to write leisurely—and possibly to read for the Bar."

" We might be together," I suggested. And Derrick took to this idea, being a man who detested solitude and crowds about equally. Since his mother's death he had been very much alone in the world. To Lawrence he was always loyal, but the two had nothing in common, and though fond of his sister he could not get on at all with the manufacturer, his brother-in-law. But this prospect of life together in London pleased him amazingly ; he began to recover his spirits to a great extent and to look much more like himself.

It must have been just as he had taken his degree that he received a telegram to announce that Major Vaughan had been invalided home, and would arrive at Southampton in three weeks' time. Derrick knew very little of his father, but apparently Mrs. Vaughan had done her best to keep up a sort of memory of his childish days at Aldershot, and in these the part that his father played was always pleasant.

B

So he looked forward to the meeting not a little, while I, from the first, had my doubts as to the felicity it was likely to bring him.

However, it was ordained that before the Major's ship arrived, his son's whole life should change. Even Lynwood was thrust into the background. As for me, I was nowhere. For Derrick, the quiet, the self-contained, had fallen passionately in love with a certain Freda Merrifield.

CHAPTER II.

"Infancy? What if the rose-streak of morning
   Pale and depart in a passion of tears?
   Once to have hoped is no matter for scorning :
   Love once : e'en love's disappointment endears,
   A moment's success pays the failure of years."

R. BROWNING.

THE wonder would have been if he had not
fallen in love with her, for a more fascinating
girl I never saw. She had only just returned
from school at Compiègne, and was not yet out;
her charming freshness was unsullied; she had
all the simplicity and straightforwardness of
unspoilt, unsophisticated girlhood. I well remember our first sight of her. We had been
invited for a fortnight's yachting by Calverley
of Exeter. His father, Sir John Calverley, had
a sailing yacht, and some guests having disappointed him at the last minute, he gave his
son *carte blanche* as to who he should bring to
fill the vacant berths.

So we three travelled down to Southampton together, one hot summer day, and were rowed out to the *Aurora*, an uncommonly neat little schooner which lay in that over-rated and frequently odoriferous roadstead, Southampton Water. However, I admit that on that evening —the tide being high—the place looked remarkably pretty ; the level rays of the setting sun turned the water to gold, a soft luminous haze hung over the town and the shipping, and by a stretch of imagination one might have thought the view almost Venetian. Derrick's perfect content was only marred by his shyness. I knew that he dreaded reaching the *Aurora;* and sure enough as we stepped on to the exquisitely white deck and caught sight of the little group of guests, I saw him retreat into his crab-shell of silent reserve. Sir John, who made a very pleasant host, introduced us to the other visitors—Lord Probyn and his wife, and their niece, Miss Freda Merrifield. Lady Probyn was Sir John's sister, and also the sister of Miss Merrifield's mother ; so that it was almost a family party, and by no means a formidable gathering. Lady Probyn played the part of hostess and chaperoned her pretty niece; but she was not in the least like the aunt of fiction —on the contrary, she was comparatively young in years and almost comically young in mind; her niece was devoted to her, and the moment I saw her I knew that our voyage could not possibly be dull.

As to Miss Freda, when we first caught sight of her she was standing near the companion, dressed in a daintily made yachting costume of blue serge and white braid, and round her white sailor hat she bore the name of the yacht stamped on a white ribbon; in her waist-band she had fastened two deep crimson roses, and she looked at us with frank, girlish curiosity, no doubt wondering whether we should add to or detract from the enjoyment of the expedition. She was rather tall, and there was an air of strength and energy about her which was most refreshing. Her skin was singularly white, but there was a healthy glow of colour in her cheeks; while her large, grey eyes, shaded by long lashes, were full of life and brightness. As to her features, they were perhaps a trifle irregular, and her elder sisters were supposed to eclipse her altogether;

but to my mind she was far the most taking of
the three.

I was not in the least surprised that Derrick
should fall head over ears in love with her ; she
was exactly the sort of girl that would infallibly
attract him.   Her absence of shyness ; her
straightforward, easy way of talking ; her genuine
good heartedness ; her devotion to animals—one
of his own pet hobbies—and finally her exquisite
playing, made the result a foregone conclusion.
And then, moreover, they were perpetually together.   He would hang over the piano in the
saloon for hours while she played, the rest of us
lazily enjoying the easy chairs and the fresh air
on deck ; and whenever we landed, these two
were sure in the end to be just a little apart from
the rest of us.

It was an eminently successful cruise.   We
all liked each other ; the sea was calm, the sun-
shine constant, the wind as a rule favourable,
and I think I never in a single fortnight heard
so many good stories, or had such a good time.
We seemed to get right out of the world and its
narrow restrictions, away from all that was
hollow and base and depressing, only landing

now and then at quaint little quiet places for some merry excursion on shore. Freda was in the highest spirits ; and as to Derrick, he was a different creature. She seemed to have the power of drawing him out in a marvellous degree, and she took the greatest interest in his work—a sure way to every author's heart.

But it was not till one day, when we landed at Tresco, that I felt certain she genuinely loved him—there in one glance the truth flashed upon me. I was walking with one of the gardeners down one of the long shady paths of that lonely little island, with its curiously foreign look, when we suddenly came face to face with Derrick and Freda. They were talking earnestly, and I could see her great grey eyes as they were lifted to his—perhaps they were more expressive than she knew—I cannot say. They both started a little as we confronted them, and the colour deepened in Freda's face. The gardener, with what photographers usually ask for—"just the faint beginning of a smile,"—turned and gathered a bit of white heather growing near.

" They say it brings good luck, miss," he remarked, handing it to Freda.

"Thank you,' she said, laughing, "I hope it will bring it to me. At any rate it will remind me of this beautiful island. Isn't it just like Paradise, Mr. Wharncliffe?"

"For me it is like Paradise before Eve was created," I replied, rather wickedly. "By the bye, are you going to keep all the good luck to yourself?"

"I don't know," she said, laughing. "Perhaps I shall; but you have only to ask the gardener, he will gather you another piece directly."

I took good care to drop behind, having no taste for the third-fiddle business; but I noticed when we were in the gig once more, rowing back to the yacht, that the white heather had been equally divided—one half was in the waist-band of the blue serge dress, the other half in the button-hole of Derrick's blazer.

So the fortnight slipped by, and at length one afternoon we found ourselves once more in Southampton Water; then came the bustle of packing and the hurry of departure, and the merry party dispersed. Derrick and I saw them all off at the station, for, as his father's ship did

not arrive till the following day, I made up my
mind to stay on with him at Southampton.

"You will come and see us in town," said
Lady Probyn, kindly.   And Lord Probyn in-
vited us both for the shooting at Blachington in
September.

"We will have the same party on shore, and
see if we can't enjoy ourselves almost as well,"
he said in his hearty way ; "the novel will go
all the better for it, eh, Vaughan ? "

Derrick brightened visibly at the suggestion.
I heard him talking to Freda all the time that
Sir John stood laughing and joking as to the
comparative pleasures of yachting and shooting.

"You will be there too ? " Derrick asked.

"I can't tell," said Freda, and there was a
shade of sadness in her tone.   Her voice was
deeper than most women's voices—a rich contralto with something striking and individual
about it.   I could hear her quite plainly ; but
Derrick spoke less distinctly—he always had a
bad trick of mumbling.

"You see I am the youngest," she said, "and
I am not really 'out.' Perhaps my mother will
wish one of the elder ones to go ; but I half

think they are already engaged for September, so after all I may have a chance."

Inaudible remark from my friend.

"Yes, I came here because my sisters did not care to leave London till the end of the season," replied the clear contralto. "It has been a perfect cruise. I shall remember it all my life."

After that, nothing more was audible ; but I imagine Derrick must have hazarded a more personal question, and that Freda had admitted that it was not only the actual sailing she should remember. At any rate her face when I caught sight of it again made me think of the girl described in the 'Biglow Papers' :

> "'Twas kin' o' kingdom come to look
> On sech a blessed creatur,
> A dogrose blushin' to a brook
> Ain't modester nor sweeter.'"

So the train went off, and Derrick and I were left to idle about Southampton and kill time as best we might. Derrick seemed to walk the streets in a sort of dream—he was perfectly well aware that he had met his fate, and at that time no thought of difficulties in the way had arisen either in his mind or in my own. We were

both of us young and inexperienced ; we were
both of us in love, and we had the usual lover's
notion that everything in heaven and earth is
prepared to favour the course of his particular
passion.

I remember that we soon found the town intolerable and, crossing by the ferry, walked over
to Netley Abbey, and lay down idly in the shade
of the old grey walls. Not a breath of wind
stirred the great masses of ivy which were
wreathed about the ruined church, and the place
looked so lovely in its decay, that we felt dis-
posed to judge the dissolute monks very leniently
for having behaved so badly that their church
and monastery had to be opened to the four
winds of heaven. After all, when is a church so
beautiful as when it has the green grass for its
floor and the sky for its roof ?

I could show you the very spot near the East
window where Derrick told me the whole truth,
and where we talked over Freda's perfections
and the probability of frequent meetings in
London. He had listened so often and so
patiently to my affairs, that it seemed an odd
reversal to have to play the confidant ; and if

now and then my thoughts wandered off to the coming month at Mondisfield, and pictured violet eyes while he talked of grey, it was not from any lack of sympathy with my friend.

Derrick was not of a self-tormenting nature, and though I knew he was amazed at the thought that such a girl as Freda could possibly care for him, yet he believed most implicitly that this wonderful thing had come to pass; and, remembering her face as we had last seen it, and the look in her eyes at Tresco, I, too, had not a shadow of a doubt that she really loved him. She was not the least bit of a flirt, and society had not had a chance yet of moulding her into the ordinary girl of the nineteenth century.

Perhaps it was the sudden and unexpected change of the next day that makes me remember Derrick's face so distinctly as he lay back on the smooth turf that afternoon in Netley Abbey. As it looked then, full of youth and hope, full of that dream of cloudless love, I never saw it again.

CHAPTER III.

" Religion in him never died, but became a habit—a habit of enduring hardness, and cleaving to the steadfast performance of duty in face of the strongest allurements to the pleasanter and easier course."—*Life of Charles Lamb*, by A. AINGER.

DERRICK was in good spirits the next day. He talked much of Major Vaughan, wondered whether the voyage home had restored his health, discussed the probable length of his leave, and speculated as to the nature of his illness ; the telegram had of course given no details.

" There hasn't been even a photograph for the last five years," he remarked, as we walked down to the quay together. " Yet I think I should know him anywhere, if it is only by his height. He used to look so well on horseback. I remember as a child seeing him in a sham fight charging up Cæsar's Camp."

" How old were you when he went out ? "

"Oh, quite a small boy," replied Derrick. "It was just before I first stayed with you. However, he has had a regular succession of photographs sent out to him, and will know me easily enough."

Poor Derrick! I can't think of that day even now without a kind of mental shiver. We watched the great steamer as it glided up to the quay, and Derrick scanned the crowded deck with eager eyes, but could nowhere see the tall, soldierly figure that had lingered so long in his memory. He stood with his hand resting on the rail of the gangway, and when presently it was raised to the side of the steamer, he still kept his position, so that he could instantly catch sight of his father as he passed down. I stood close behind him, and watched the motley procession of passengers ; most of them had the dull, colourless skin which bespeaks long residence in India, and a particularly yellow and peevish-looking old man was grumbling loudly as he slowly made his way down the gangway.

"The most disgraceful scene!" he remarked. "The fellow was as drunk as he could be."

"Who was it?" asked his companion.

"Why, Major Vaughan, to be sure. The only wonder is that he hasn't drunk himself to death by this time—been at it years enough!"

Derrick turned, as though to shelter himself from the curious eyes of the travellers; but everywhere the quay was crowded. It seemed to me not unlike the life that lay before him, with this new shame which could not be hid, and I shall never forget the look of misery in his face.

"Most likely a great exaggeration of that spiteful old fogey's," I said. "'Never believe anything that you hear,' is a sound axiom. Had you not better try to get on board?"

"Yes; and for heaven's sake come with me, Wharncliffe!" he said. "It can't be true! It is, as you say, that man's spite, or else there is some one else of the name on board. That must be it—some one else of the name."

I don't know whether he managed to deceive himself. We made our way on board, and he spoke to one of the stewards, who conducted us to the saloon. I knew from the expression of the man's face that the words we had overheard were but too true; it was a mere glance that he

gave us, yet if he had said aloud, " They belong
to that old drunkard! Thank Heaven I'm not
in their shoes!" I could not have better understood what was in his mind.

There were three persons only in the great
saloon : an officer's servant, whose appearance
did not please me; a fine-looking old man with
grey hair and whiskers, and a rough-hewn honest
face, apparently the ship's doctor; and a tall
grizzled man, in whom I at once saw a sort of
horrible likeness to Derrick—horrible because
this face was wicked and degraded, and because
its owner was drunk—noisily drunk.

Derrick paused for a minute, looking at his
father; then, deadly pale, he turned to the old
doctor. " I am Major Vaughan's son," he said.

The doctor grasped his hand, and there was
something in the old man's kindly, chivalrous
manner which brought a sort of light into the
gloom.

" I am very glad to see you!" he exclaimed.
" Is the Major's luggage ready?" he inquired,
turning to the servant. Then, as the man replied in the affirmative, " How would it be, Mr.
Vaughan, if your father's man just saw the

things into a cab ? and then I'll come on shore
with you and see my patient safely settled in."

Derrick acquiesced, and the doctor turned to
the Major, who was leaning up against one of
the pillars of the saloon and shouting out "'Twas
in Trafalgar Bay" in a way which, under other
circumstances, would have been highly comic.
The doctor interrupted him, as with much feeling he sang how—

> " England declared that every man
> That day had done his duty."

"Look, Major," he said ; "here is your son
come to meet you."

"Glad to see you, my boy," said the Major,
reeling forward and running all his words together. "How's your mother ? Is this Lawrence ? Glad to see both of you ! Why, you'r's
like's two peas ! Not Lawrence, do you say ?
Confound it, doctor, how the ship rolls to-day ! "

And the old wretch staggered and would have
fallen, had not Derrick supported him and landed
him safely on one of the fixed ottomans.

"Yes, yes, you're the son for me," he went on,
with a bland smile, which made his face all the

c

more hideous. "You're not so rough and clumsy as that confounded John Thomas, whose hands are like brickbats. I'm a mere wreck, as you see; it's the accursed climate! But your mother will soon nurse me into health again; she was always a good nurse, poor soul! it was her best point. What with you and your mother, I shall soon be myself again."

Here the doctor interposed, and Derrick made desperately for a porthole and gulped down mouthfuls of fresh air: but he was not allowed much of a respite, for the servant returned to say that he had procured a cab, and the Major called loudly for his son's arm.

"I'll not have you," he said, pushing the servant violently away. "Come, Derrick, help me! you are worth two of that blockhead."

And Derrick came quickly forward, his face still very pale, but with a dignity about it which I had never before seen; and, giving his arm to his drunken father, he piloted him across the saloon, through the staring ranks of stewards, officials, and tardy passengers outside, down the gangway, and over the crowded quay to the cab. I knew that each derisive glance of the specta-

tors was to him like a sword-thrust, and longed
to throttle the Major, who seemed to enjoy himself amazingly on *terra firma*, and sang at the
top of his voice as we drove through the streets
of Southampton. The old doctor kept up a
cheery flow of small-talk with me, thinking, no
doubt, that this would be a kindness to Derrick:
and at last that purgatorial drive ended and
somehow Derrick and the Doctor between them
got the Major safely into his room at Radley's
Hotel.

We had ordered lunch in a private sitting-
room, thinking that the Major would prefer it to
the coffee-room ; but, as it turned out, he was in
no state to appear. They left him asleep, and the
ship's doctor sat in the seat that had been prepared for his patient, and made the meal as
tolerable to us both as it could be. He was an
odd, old-fashioned fellow, but as true a gentle-
man as ever breathed.

" Now," he said, when lunch was over, " you
and I must just have a talk together, Mr.
Vaughan, and I will help you to understand
your father's case."

I made a movement to go, but sat down again

at Derrick's request. I think, poor old fellow, he dreaded being alone, and knowing that I had seen his father at the worst, thought I might as well hear all particulars.

" Major Vaughan," continued the doctor, " has now been under my care for some weeks, and I had some communication with the regimental surgeon about his case before he sailed. He is suffering from an enlarged liver, and the disease has been brought on by his unfortunate habit of over-indulgence in stimulants." I could almost have smiled, so very gently and considerately did the good old man veil in long words the shameful fact. " It is a habit sadly prevalent among our fellow-countrymen in India; the climate aggravates the mischief, and very many lives are in this way ruined. Then your father was also unfortunate enough to contract rheumatism when he was camping out in the jungle last year, and this is increasing on him very much, so that his life is almost intolerable to him, and he naturally flies for relief to his greatest enemy, drink. At all costs, however, you must keep him from stimulants; they will only intensify the disease and the sufferings, in fact they are poison to a man in such a state. Don't think I am a bigot in these matters; but I say that for a man in such a condition as this, there is nothing for it but total abstinence, and at all costs your father must be guarded from the possibility of procuring any sort of intoxicating drink. Throughout the voyage I have done my best to shield him, but it was a difficult matter. His servant, too, is not trustworthy, and should be dismissed if possible."

"Had he spoken at all of his plans?" asked Derrick, and his voice sounded strangely unlike itself.

"He asked me what place in England he had better settle down in," said the doctor, "and I strongly recommended him to try Bath. This seemed to please him, and if he is well enough he had better go there to-morrow. He mentioned your mother this morning; no doubt she will know how to manage him."

"My mother died six months ago," said Derrick, pushing back his chair and beginning to pace the room. The doctor made kindly apologies.

"Perhaps you have a sister, who could go to him?"

"No," replied Derrick. "My only sister is married, and her husband would never allow it."

"Or a cousin or an aunt?" suggested the old man, naively unconscious that the words sounded like a quotation.

I saw the ghost of a smile flit over Derrick's harassed face as he shook his head.

"I suggested that he should go into some Home for—cases of the kind," resumed the doctor, "or place himself under the charge of some medical man; however, he won't hear of such a thing. But if he is left to himself—well, it is all up with him. He will drink himself to death in a few months."

"He shall not be left alone," said Derrick; "I will live with him. Do you think I should do? It seems to be Hobson's choice."

I looked up in amazement—for here was Derrick calmly giving himself up to a life that must crush every plan for the future he had made. Did men make such a choice as that while they took two or three turns in a room? Did they speak so composedly after a struggle that must have been so bitter? Thinking it over now, I feel sure it was his extraordinary gift of insight and his clear judgment which made him behave in this way. He instantly perceived and promptly acted ; the worst of the suffering came long after.

" Why, of course you are the very best person in the world for him," said the doctor. " He has taken a fancy to you, and evidently you have a certain influence with him. If any one can save him it will be you."

But the thought of allowing Derrick to be sacrificed to that old brute of a Major was more than I could bear calmly.

" A more mad scheme was never proposed," I cried. " Why, doctor, it will be utter ruin to my friend's career ; he will lose years that no one can ever make up. And besides, he is unfit for such a strain ; he will never stand it."

My heart felt hot as I thought of Derrick, with his highly-strung, sensitive nature, his refinement, his gentleness, in constant companionship with such a man as Major Vaughan.

" My dear sir," said the old doctor, with a gleam in his eye, " I understand your feeling well enough. But depend upon it, your friend has made the right choice, and there is no

doubt that he'll be strong enough to do his
duty."

The word reminded me of the Major's song,
and my voice was abominably sarcastic in tone
as I said to Derrick, " You no longer consider
writing your duty then ? "

" Yes," he said, " but it must stand second to
this. Don't be vexed, Sydney ; our plans are
knocked on the head, but it is not so bad as
you make out. I have at any rate enough to
live on, and can afford to wait."

There was no more to be said, and the next
day I saw that strange trio set out on their road
to Bath. The Major looking more wicked when
sober than he had done when drunk ; the
old doctor kindly and considerate as ever ;
and Derrick, with an air of resolution about
that English face of his, and a dauntless
expression in his eyes which impressed me
curiously.

These quiet reserved fellows are always giving
one odd surprises. He had astonished me by
the vigour and depth of the first volume of
" Lynwood's Heritage." He astonished me now
by a new phase in his own character. Appar-

ently he who had always been content to follow where I led, and to watch life rather than to take an active share in it, now intended to strike out a very decided line of his own.

CHAPTER IV.

"Both Goethe and Schiller were profoundly convinced that Art was no luxury of leisure, no mere amusement to charm the idle, or relax the careworn ; but a mighty influence, serious in its aims although pleasureable in its means ; a sister of Religion, by whose aid the great world-scheme was wrought into reality."
—LEWES'S *Life of Goethe.*

MAN is a selfish being, and I am a particularly fine specimen of the race as far as that characteristic goes. If I had had a dozen drunken parents I should never have danced attendance on one of them ; yet in my secret soul I admired Derrick for the line he had taken, for we mostly do admire what is unlike ourselves and really noble, though it is the fashion to seem totally indifferent to everything in heaven and earth. But all the same I felt annoyed about the whole business, and was glad to forget it in my own affairs at Mondisfield.

Weeks passed by. I lived through a midsummer dream of happiness, and a hard awaking. That, however, has nothing to do with Derrick's story, and may be passed over. In October I settled down in Montague Street, Bloomsbury, and began to read for the Bar, in about as disagreeable a frame of mind as can be conceived. One morning I found on my breakfast table a letter in Derrick's handwriting. Like most men we hardly ever corresponded—what women say in the eternal letters they send to each other I can't conceive—but it struck me that under the circumstances I ought to have sent him a line to ask how he was getting on, and my conscience pricked me as I remembered that I had hardly thought of him since we parted, being absorbed in my own matters. The letter was not very long, but when one read between the lines it somehow told a good deal. I have it lying by me, and this is a copy of it.

" DEAR SYDNEY,—Do like a good fellow go to North Audley Street for me, to the house which I described to you as the one where Lynwood lodged, and tell me what he would see besides the church from his window—if shops, what kind ? Also if any glimpse of Oxford Street would be visible. Then if you'll add to your favours by getting me a second-hand copy of Laveleye's ' Socialisme Contemporain,' I should be for ever grateful. We are settled in here all right. Bath is empty, but I people it as far as I can with the folk out of 'Evelina' and 'Persuasion.' How did you get on at Blachington? and which of the Misses Merrifield went in the end? Don't bother about the commissions. Any time will do.

"Ever yours,

"DERRICK VAUGHAN."

Poor old fellow! all the spirit seemed knocked out of him. There was not one word about the Major, and who could say what wretchedness was veiled in that curt phrase, "we are settled in all right"? All right! it was all as wrong as it could be! My blood began to boil at the thought of Derrick, with his great powers—his wonderful gift—cooped up in a place where the study of life was so limited and so dull. Then there was his hunger for news of Freda, and his silence as to what had kept him away from Blachington, and about all a sort of proud humility which prevented him from saying much that I should have expected him to say under the circumstances.

It was Saturday, and my time was my own. I went out, got his book for him; interviewed North Audley Street; spent a bad five minutes

in company with that villain " Bradshaw," who is
responsible for so much of the brain and eye
disease of the nineteenth century, and finally left
Paddington in the Flying Dutchman, which
landed me at Bath early in the afternoon.   I
left my portmanteau at the station, and walked
through the city till I reached Gay Street.   Like
most of the streets of Bath, it was broad, and
had on either hand dull, well-built, dark grey,
eminently respectable, unutterably dreary-look-
ing houses.   I rang, and the door was opened
to me by a most quaint old woman, evidently
the landlady.   An odour of curry pervaded the
passage, and became more oppressive as the
door of the sitting-room was opened, and I was
ushered in upon the Major and his son, who had
just finished lunch.

"Hullo !" cried Derrick, springing up, his face
full of delight which touched me, while at the
same time it filled me with envy.

Even the Major thought fit to give me a
hearty welcome.

"Glad to see you again," he said pleasantly
enough.   " It's a relief to have a fresh face to
look at.   We have a room which is quite at your

disposal, and I hope you'll stay with us.   Brought
your portmanteau, eh ? "

" It is at the station," I replied.

" See that it is sent for," he said to Derrick ;
"and show Mr. Wharncliffe all that is to be seen
in this cursed hole of a place." Then, turning
again to me, " Have you lunched ? Very well,
then, don't waste this fine afternoon in an invalid's room, but be off and enjoy yourself."

So cordial was the old man, that I should
have thought him already a reformed character,
had I not found that he kept the rough side of
his tongue for home use.   Derrick placed a
novel and a small hand-bell within his reach,
and we were just going, when we were checked
by a volley of oaths from the Major ; then a
book came flying across the room, well-aimed at
Derrick's head.   He stepped aside, and let it fall
with a crash on the sideboard.

" What do you mean by giving me the second
volume when you know I am in the third ? "
fumed the invalid.

He apologised quietly, fetched the third
volume, straightened the disordered leaves of
the discarded second, and with the air of one

well accustomed to such little domestic scenes, took up his hat and came out with me.

" How long do you intend to go on playing David to the Major's Saul?" I asked, marvelling at the way in which he endured the humours of his father.

" As long as I have the chance," he replied. " I say, are you sure you won't mind staying with us ?   It can't be a very comfortable household for an outsider."

"Much better than for an insider, to all appearance," I replied.   " I'm only too delighted to stay.   And now, old fellow, tell me the honest truth—you didn't, you know, in your letter— how have you been getting on ? "

Derrick launched into an account of his father's ailments.

" Oh, hang the Major !   I don't care about him, I want to know about you," I cried.

"About me?" said Derrick, doubtfully.   "Oh, I'm right enough ? "

" What do you do with yourself?   How on earth do you kill time ? " I asked.   " Come, give me a full, true, and particular account of it all."

" We have tried three other servants," said

Derrick; "but the plan doesn't answer. They either won't stand it, or else they are bribed into smuggling brandy into the house. I find I can do most things for my father, and in the morning he has an attendant from the hospital who is trustworthy, and who does what is necessary for him. At ten we breakfast together, then there are the morning papers which he likes to have read to him. After that I go round to the Pump Room with him—odd contrast now to what it must have been when Bath was the rage. Then we have lunch. In the afternoon, if he is well enough, we drive; if not, he sleeps, and I get a walk. Later on an old Indian friend of his will sometimes drop in; if not, he likes to be read to until dinner. After dinner we play chess—he is a first-rate player. At ten I help him to bed; from eleven to twelve I smoke and study Socialism and all the rest of it that Lynwood is at present floundering in."

"Why don't you write then?"

"I tried it, but it didn't answer. I couldn't sleep after it, and was in fact too tired; seems absurd to be tired after such a day as that, but somehow it takes it out of one more than the hardest reading; I don't know why."

"Why," I said, angrily, "it's because it is work to which you are quite unsuited—work for a thick-skinned, hard-hearted, uncultivated and well-paid attendant, not for the novelist who is to be the chief light of our generation."

He laughed at this estimate of his powers.

"Novelists, like other cattle, have to obey their owner," he said lightly.

I thought for a moment that he meant the Major, and was breaking into an angry remonstrance, when I saw that he meant something quite different. It was always his strongest point, this extraordinary consciousness of right, this unwavering belief that he had to do and therefore could do certain things. Without this, I know that he never wrote a line, and in my heart I believe that this was the cause of his success.

"Then you are not writing at all?" I asked.

"Yes, I write generally for a couple of hours before breakfast," he said.

And that evening we sat by his gas stove and

D

he read me the next four chapters of " Lynwood." He had rather a dismal lodging-house
bed-room, with faded wall-paper and prosaic
snuff-coloured carpet. On a rickety table in the
window was his desk, and a portfolio full of blue
foolscap, but he had done what he could to make
the place habitable; his Oxford pictures were
on the walls—Hoffmann's " Christ speaking to
the Woman taken in Adultery " hanging over
the mantelpiece—it had always been a favourite
of his. I remember that, as he read the description of Lynwood and his wife, I kept looking
from him to the Christ in the picture, till I could
almost have fancied that each face bore the same
expression. Had his strange monotonous life
with that old brute of a Major brought him some
new perception of those words, " Neither do I
condemn thee?" But when he stopped reading,
I, true to my character, forgot his affairs in my
own, and we sat talking far into the night—talking of that luckless month at Mondisfield, of all
the problems it had opened up, and of my
wretchedness.

"You were in town all September?" he asked;
" you gave up Blachington ?"

"Yes," I replied. "What did I care for country houses in such a mood as that?"

He acquiesced, and I went on talking of my grievances, and it was not till I was in the train, on my way back to London, that I remembered how a look of disappointment had passed over his face just at the moment. Evidently he had counted on learning something about Freda from me, and I—well, I had clean forgotten both her existence and his passionate love.

. Something, probably self-interest, the desire for my friend's company, and so forth, took me down to Bath pretty frequently in those days ; luckily the Major had a sort of liking for me, and was always polite enough ; and dear old Derrick—well, I believe my visits really helped to brighten him up. At any rate he said he couldn't have borne his life without them, and for a sceptical, dismal, cynical fellow like me to hear that was somehow flattering. The mere force of contrast did me good. I used to come back on the Monday wondering that Derrick didn't cut his throat, and realizing that, after all, it was something to be a free agent, and to have comfortable rooms in Montague Street, with no

old bear of a drunkard to disturb my peace.
And then a sort of admiration sprang up in my
heart, and the cynicism bred of melancholy
broodings over solitary pipes was less rampant
than usual.

It was, I think, early in the new year that I
met Lawrence Vaughan in Bath.   He was not
staying at Gay Street, so I could still have the
vacant room next to Derrick's.   Lawrence put
up at the York House Hotel.

" For you know," he informed me, " I really
can't stand the governor for more than an hour
or two at a time."

" Derrick manages to do it," I said.

" Oh, Derrick, yes," he replied, "it's his *métier*,
and he is well accustomed to the life.   Besides,
you know, he is such a dreamy, quiet sort of
fellow ; he lives all the time in a world of his
own creation, and bears the discomforts of this
world with great philosophy.   Actually he has
turned teetotaler !   It would kill me in a week."

I make a point of never arguing with a fellow
like that, but I think I had a vindictive longing,
as I looked at him, to shut him up with the
Major for a month, and see what would happen.

These twin brothers were curiously alike in face and curiously unlike in nature. So much for the great science of physiognomy! It often seemed to me that they were the complement of each other. For instance, Derrick in society was extremely silent, Lawrence was a rattling talker; Derrick, when alone with you, would now and then reveal unsuspected depths of thought and expression; Lawrence, when alone with you, very frequently showed himself to be a cad. The elder twin was modest and diffident, the younger inclined to brag; the one had a strong tendency to melancholy, the other was blest or curst with the sort of temperament which has been said to accompany "a hard heart and a good digestion."

I was not surprised to find that the son who could not tolerate the governor's presence for more than an hour or two, was a prime favourite with the old man : that was just the way of the world. Of course, the Major was as polite as possible to him ; Derrick got the kicks and Lawrence the halfpence.

In the evenings we played whist, Lawrence coming in after dinner, " For you know," he explained to me, " I really couldn't get through a meal with nothing but those infernal mineral waters to wash it down."

And here I must own that at my first visit I had sailed rather close to the wind; for when the Major, like the Hatter in " Alice," pressed me to take wine, I—not seeing any—had answered that I did not take it ; mentally adding the words, " in your house, you brute ! "

The two brothers were fond of each other after a fashion. But Derrick was human, and had his faults like the rest of us ; and I am pretty sure he did not much enjoy the sight of his father's foolish and unreasoning devotion to Lawrence. If you come to think of it, he would have been a full-fledged angel if no jealous pang, no reflection that it was rather rough on him, had crossed his mind, when he saw his younger brother treated with every mark of respect and liking, and knew that Lawrence would never stir a finger really to help the poor fractious invalid. Unluckily they happened one night to get on the subject of professions.

"It's a comfort," said the Major in his sarcastic way, "to have a fellow soldier to talk to instead

of a quill-driver, who as yet is not even a penny-
a-liner.   Eh, Derrick?   Don't you feel inclined
to regret your fool's choice now?   You might
have been starting off for the war with Lawrence
next week, if you hadn't chosen what you're
pleased to call a literary life.   Literary life,
indeed! I little thought a son of mine would
ever have been so wanting in spirit as to prefer
dabbling in ink to a life of action—to be the
scribbler of mere words, rather than an officer of
dragoons."

Then to my astonishment Derrick sprang to
his feet in hot indignation.   I never saw him
look so handsome, before or since; for his anger
was not the distorting devilish anger that the
Major gave way to, but real downright wrath.

"You speak contemptuously of mere novels,"
he said in a low voice, yet more clearly than
usual and as if the words were wrung out of
him.   "What right have you to look down on
one of the greatest weapons of the day? and
why is a writer to submit to scoffs and insults
and tamely to hear his profession reviled?   I
have chosen to write the message that has been
given me, and I don't regret the choice.   Should

I have shown greater spirit if I had sold my
freedom and right of judgment to be one of the
national killing machines ? "

With that he threw down his cards and strode
out of the room in a white heat of anger.   It
was a pity he made that last remark, for it put
him in the wrong and needlessly annoyed Lawrence and the Major.   But an angry man has no
time to weigh his words, and, as I said,
poor old Derrick was very human, and when
wounded too intolerably could on occasion re-
taliate.

The Major uttered an oath and looked in
astonishment at the retreating figure.   Derrick
was such an extraordinarily quiet, respectful, long-
suffering son as a rule, that this outburst was
startling in the extreme.   Moreover, it spoilt
the game, and the old man, chafed by the result
of his own ill-nature, and helpless to bring back
his partner, was forced to betake himself to chess.
I left him grumbling away to Lawrence about
the vanity of authors, and went out in the hope of
finding Derrick.   As I left the house I saw
someone turn the corner into the Circus, and
starting in pursuit, overtook the tall dark figure

where Bennett Street opens on to the Lansdowne Hill.

"I'm glad you spoke up, old fellow," I said, taking his arm.

He modified his pace a little. "Why is it," he exclaimed, "that every other profession can be taken seriously, but that a novelist's work is supposed to be mere play? Good God! don't we suffer enough? Have we not hard brain work and drudgery of desk work and tedious gathering of statistics and troublesome search into details? Have we not an appalling weight of responsibility on us?—and are we not at the mercy of a thousand capricious chances?"

"Come now," I exclaimed, "you know that you are never so happy as when you are writing."

"Of course," he replied; "but that doesn't make me resent such an attack the less. Besides, you don't know what it is to have to write in such an atmosphere as ours; it's like a weight on one's pen. This life here is not life at all—it's a daily death, and it's killing the book too; the last chapters are wretched, I'm utterly dissatisfied with them."

"As for that," I said calmly, "you are no

judge at all. You never can tell the worth of your own work ; the last bit is splendid."

"I could have done it better," he groaned. "But there is always a ghastly depression dragging one back here—and then the time is so short; just as one gets into the swing of it the breakfast bell rings, and then comes——" He broke off.

I could well supply the end of the sentence, however, for I knew that then came the slow torture of a *tête-à-tête* day with the Major, stinging sarcasms, humiliating scoldings, vexations and difficulties innumerable.

I drew him to the left, having no mind to go to the top of the hill. We slackened our pace again and walked to and fro along the broad level pavement of Lansdowne Crescent. We had it entirely to ourselves—not another creature was in sight.

"I could bear it all," he burst forth, "if only there was a chance of seeing Freda. Oh, you are better off than I am—at least you know the worst. Your hope is killed, but mine lives on a tortured, starved life ! Would to God I had never seen her ! "

Certainly before that night I had never quite realized the irrevocableness of poor Derrick's passion. I had half hoped that time and separation would gradually efface Freda Merrifield from his memory; and I listened with a dire foreboding to the flood of wretchedness which he poured forth as we paced up and down, thinking now and then how little people guessed at the tremendous powers hidden under his usually quiet exterior.

At length he paused, but his last heart-broken words seemed to vibrate in the air and to force me to speak some kind of comfort.

"Derrick," I said, "come back with me to London—give up this miserable life."

I felt him start a little; evidently no thought of yielding had come to him before. We were passing the house that used to belong to that strange book-lover and recluse, Beckford. I looked up at the blank windows, and thought of that curious, self-centred life in the past, surrounded by every luxury, able to indulge every whim; and then I looked at my companion's pale, tortured face, and thought of the life he had elected to lead in the hope of saving one whom duty bound him to honour.   After all, which life was the most worth living—which was the most to be admired ?

We walked on : down below us and up on the further hill we could see the lights of Bath ; the place so beautiful by day looked now like a fairy city, and the Abbey, looming up against the moon-lit sky, seemed like some great giant keeping watch over the clustering roofs below. The well-known chimes rang out into the night and the clock struck ten.

" I must go back," said Derrick quietly.   " My father will want to get to bed."

I couldn't say a word ; we turned, passed Beckford's house once more, walked briskly down the hill, and reached the Gay Street lodging-house.   I remember the stifling heat of the room as we entered it, and its contrast to the cool, dark, winter's night outside.   I can vividly recall, too, the old Major's face as he looked up with a sarcastic remark, but with a shade of anxiety in his bloodshot eyes.   He was leaning back in a green-cushioned chair, and his ghastly yellow complexion seemed to me more noticeable than usual—his scanty grey hair and whiskers, the lines of pain so plainly visible in his face, impressed me curiously. I think I had never before realized what a wreck of a man he was—how utterly dependent on others.

Lawrence, who, to do him justice, had a good deal of tact, and who, I believe, cared for his brother as much as he was capable of caring for anyone but himself, repeated a good story with which he had been enlivening the Major, and I did what I could to keep up the talk. Derrick meanwhile put away the chessmen, and lighted the Major's candle. He even managed to force up a laugh at Lawrence's story, and, as he helped his father out of the room, I think I was the only one who noticed the look of tired endurance in his eyes.

CHAPTER V.

"I know
How far high failure overtops the bounds
Of low successes. Only suffering draws
The inner heart of song, and can elicit
The perfumes of the soul."—*Epic of Hades.*

NEXT week, Lawrence went off like a hero to the war; and my friend—also I think like a hero—stayed on at Bath, enduring as best he could the worst form of loneliness; for undoubtedly there is no loneliness so frightful as constant companionship with an uncongenial person. He had, however, one consolation: the Major's health steadily improved, under the joint influence of total abstinence and Bath waters, and, with the improvement, his temper became a little better.

But one Saturday, when I had run down to Bath without writing beforehand, I suddenly found a different state of things. In Orange

Grove I met Dr. Mackrill, the Major's medical man ; he used now and then to play whist with us on Saturday nights, and I stopped to speak to him.

"Oh! you've come down again. That's all right!" he said. "Your friend wants someone to cheer him up. He's got his arm broken."

"How on earth did he manage that," I asked.

"Well, that's more than I can tell you," said the Doctor, with an odd look in his eyes, as if he guessed more than he would put into words. "All that I could get out of him was that it was done accidentally. The Major is not so well— no whist for us to-night, I'm afraid."

He passed on, and I made my way to Gay Street. There was an air of mystery about the quaint old landlady ; she looked brimful of news when she opened the door to me, but she managed to "keep herself to herself," and showed me in upon the Major and Derrick, rather triumphantly I thought. The Major looked terribly ill— worse than I had ever seen him, and, as for Derrick, he had the strangest look of shrinking and shame-facedness you ever saw. He said he was glad to see me, but I knew that he lied

He would have given anything to have kept me away.

"Broken your arm?" I exclaimed, feeling bound to take some notice of the sling.

"Yes," he replied, "I met with an accident to it. But luckily it's only the left one, so it doesn't hinder me much! I have finished seven chapters of the last volume of 'Lynwood,' and was just wanting to ask you a legal question."

All this time his eyes bore my scrutiny defiantly; they seemed to dare me to say one other word about the broken arm. I didn't dare—indeed to this day I have never mentioned the subject to him.

But that evening, while he was helping the Major to bed, the old landlady made some pretext for toiling up to the top of the house, where I sat smoking in Derrick's room.

"You'll excuse my making bold to speak to you, sir," she said. I threw down my newspaper, and, looking up, saw that she was bubbling over with some story.

"Well?" I said, encouragingly.

"It's about Mr. Vaughan, sir, I wanted to speak to you. I really do think, sir, it's not

safe he should be left alone with his father, sir,
any longer. Such doings as we had here the
other day, sir! Somehow or other—and none
of us can't think how—the Major had managed
to get hold of a bottle of brandy. How he had
it I don't know ; but we none of us suspected
him, and in the afternoon he says he was too
poorly to go for a drive or to go out in his chair,
and settles off on the parlour sofa for a nap
while Mr. Vaughan goes out for a walk. Mr.
Vaughan was out a couple of hours. I heard
him come in and go into the sitting-room ; then
there came sounds of voices, and a scuffling of
feet and moving of chairs, and I knew something was wrong and hurried up to the door—
and just then came a crash like fire-irons, and I
could hear the Major a-swearing fearful. Not
hearing a sound from Mr. Vaughan, I got
scared, sir, and opened the door, and there I
saw the Major a-leaning up against the mantelpiece as drunk as a lord, and his son seemed to
have got the bottle from him ; it was half empty,
and when he saw me he just handed it to me
and ordered me to take it away. Then between
us we got the Major to lie down on the sofa and

E

left him there. When we got out into the passage Mr. Vaughan he leant against the wall for
a minute, looking as white as a sheet, and then
I noticed for the first time that his left arm was
hanging down at his side. 'Lord! sir,' I cried,
'your arm's broken.' And he went all at once
as red as he had been pale just before, and said
he had got it done accidentally, and bade me
say nothing about it, and walked off there and
then to the doctor's, and had it set. But, sir,
given a man drunk as the Major was, and given
a scuffle to get away the drink that was poison-
ing him, and given a crash such as I heard, and
given a poker a-lying in the middle of the room
where it stands to reason no poker could get
unless it was thrown—why, sir, no sensible
woman who can put two and two together can
doubt that it was all the Major's doing."

"Yes," I said, "that is clear enough ; but for
Mr. Vaughan's sake we must hush it up ; and, as
for safety, why, the Major is hardly strong
enough to do him any worse damage than
that."

The good old thing wiped away a tear from
her eyes. She was very fond of Derrick, and it

went to her heart that he should lead such a dog's life.

I said what I could to comfort her, and she went down again, fearful lest he should discover her upstairs and guess that she had opened her heart to me.

Poor Derrick! That he of all people on earth should be mixed up with such a police-court story—with drunkards, and violence, and pokers figuring in it! I lay back in the camp chair and looked at Hoffman's "Christ," and thought of all the extraordinary problems that one is for ever coming across in life. And I wondered whether the people of Bath who saw the tall, impassive-looking, hazel-eyed son and the invalid father in their daily pilgrimages to the Pump Room, or in church on Sunday, or in the Park on sunny afternoons, had the least notion of the tragedy that was going on. My reflections were interrupted by his entrance. He had forced up a cheerfulness that I am sure he didn't really feel, and seemed afraid of letting our talk flag for a moment. I remember, too, that for the first time he offered to read me his novel, instead of as usual waiting for me to ask to hear it. I can see him now, fetching the untidy portfolio and turning over the pages, adroitly enough, as though anxious to show how immaterial was the loss of a left arm. That night I listened to the first half of the third volume of "Lynwood's Heritage," and couldn't help reflecting that its author seemed to thrive on misery; and yet how I grudged him to this deadly-lively place, and this monotonous, cooped-up life.

"How do you manage to write one-handed?" I asked.

And he sat down to his desk, put a letter-weight on the left-hand corner of the sheet of foolscap, and wrote that comical first paragraph of the eighth chapter over which we have all laughed. I suppose few readers guessed the author's state of mind when he wrote it. I looked over his shoulder to see what he had written, and couldn't help laughing aloud,—I verily believe that it was his way of turning off attention from his arm, and leading me safely from the region of awkward questions.

"By-the-bye," I exclaimed, "your writing of garden-parties reminds me. I went to one at

Campden Hill the other day, and had the good
fortune to meet Miss Freda Merrifield."

How his face lighted up, poor fellow, and
what a flood of questions he poured out. " She
looked very well and very pretty," I replied. " I
played two sets of tennis with her. She asked
after you directly she saw me, seeming to think
that we always hunted in couples. I told her
you were living here, taking care of an invalid
father ; but just then up came the others to
arrange the game. She and I got the best
courts, and as we crossed over to them she told
me she had met your brother several times last
autumn, when she had been staying near Aldershot. Odd that he never mentioned her here ;
but I don't suppose she made much impression
on him, She is not at all his style."

"Did you have much more talk with her ? "
he asked.

" No, nothing to be called talk. She told me
they were leaving London next week, and she
was longing to get back to the country to her
beloved animals—rabbits, poultry, an aviary, and
all that kind of thing. I should gather that they
had kept her rather in the background this

season, but I understand that the eldest sister is
to be married in the winter, and then no doubt
Miss Freda will be brought forward."

He seemed wonderfully cheered by this oppor-
tune meeting, and though there was so little to
tell he appeared to be quite content. I left him
on Monday in fairly good spirits, and did not
come across him again till September, when his
arm was well, and his novel finished and revised.
He never made two copies of his work, and I
fancy this was perhaps because he spent so short
a time each day in actual writing, and lived so
continually in his work ; moreover, as I said before, he detested penmanship.

The last part of " Lynwood " far exceeded my
expectations ; perhaps—yet I don't really think
so—I viewed it too favourably.   But I owed the
book a debt of gratitude, since it certainly
helped me through the worst part of my life.

" Don't you feel flat now it is finished ? " I
asked.

" I felt so miserable that I had to plunge into
another story three days after," he replied ; and
then and there he gave me the sketch of his
second novel, " At Strife," and told me how he

meant to weave in his childish fancies about the defence of the bridge in the Civil Wars.

"And about 'Lynwood?' Are you coming up to town to hawk him round?" I asked.

"I can't do that," he said; "you see I am tied here. No, I must send him off by rail, and let him take his chance."

"No such thing!" I cried. "If you can't leave Bath I will take him round for you."

And Derrick, who with the oddest inconsistency would let his MS. lie about anyhow at home, but hated the thought of sending it out alone on its travels, gladly accepted my offer. So next week I set off with the huge brown paper parcel; few, however, will appreciate my good nature, for no one but an author or a publisher knows the fearful weight of a three volume novel in MS.! To my intense satisfaction I soon got rid of it, for the first good firm to which I took it received it with great politeness, to be handed over to their "reader" for an opinion; and apparently the "reader's" opinion coincided with mine, for a month later Derrick received an offer for it with which he at once closed—not because it was a good one, but be-

cause the firm was well thought of, and because
he wished to lose no time, but to have the book
published at once. I happened to be there when
his first "proofs" arrived. The Major had had
an attack of jaundice, and was in a fiendish
humour. We had a miserable time of it at
dinner, for he badgered Derrick almost past
bearing, and I think the poor old fellow minded it
more when there was a third person present.
Somehow, through all, he managed to keep his
extraordinary capacity for reverencing mere age
—even this degraded and detestable old age of
the Major's. I often thought that in this he was
like my own ancestor, Hugo Wharncliffe, whose
deference and respectfulness and patience, had
not descended to me, while unfortunately the
effects of his physical infirmities had. I sometimes used to reflect bitterly enough on the truth
of Herbert Spencer's teaching as to heredity, so
clearly shown in my own case. In the year 1683,
through the abominable cruelty and harshness
of his brother Randolph, this Hugo Wharncliffe,
my   great-great-great-great-great grandfather,
was immured in Newgate, and his constitution
was thereby so much impaired and enfeebled

that, two hundred years after, my constitution is paying the penalty, and my whole life is thereby changed and thwarted. Hence this childless Randolph is affecting the course of several lives in the 19th century to their grievous hurt.

But *revenons à nos moutons*—that is to say, to our lion and lamb—the old brute of a Major and his long-suffering son.

While the table was being cleared, the Major took forty winks on the sofa, and we two beat a retreat, lit up our pipes in the passage, and were just turning out when the postman's double knock came, but no shower of letters in the box. Derrick threw open the door, and the man handed him a fat stumpy-looking roll in a pink wrapper.

" I say ! " he exclaimed, "*proofs !* "

And, in hot haste, he began tearing away the pink paper, till out came the clean, folded bits of printing and the dirty and dishevelled blue foolscap, the look of which I knew so well. It is an odd feeling, that first seeing oneself in print, and I could guess, even then, what a thrill shot through Derrick as he turned over the pages. But he would not take them into the sitting-room, no doubt dreading another diatribe against his profession ; and we solemnly played euchre, and patiently endured the Major's withering sarcasms till ten o'clock sounded our happy release.

However, to make a long story short, a month later—that is, at the end of November—" Lynwood's Heritage " was published, in three volumes with maroon cloth and gilt lettering. Derrick had distributed among his friends the publishers' announcement of the day of publication ; and when it was out I besieged the libraries for it, always expressing surprise if I did not find it in their lists. Then began the time of reviews. As I had expected, they were extremely favourable, with the exception of *The Herald*, *The Stroller*, and *The Hour*, which made it rather hot for him, the latter in particular pitching into his views and assuring its readers that the book was " dangerous," and its author a believer in—various things especially repugnant to Derrick, as it happened.

I was with him when he read these reviews. Over the cleverness of the satirical attack in *The Weekly Herald* he laughed heartily, though

the laugh was against himself; and as to the
critic who wrote in the *Stroller* it was apparent
to all who knew "Lynwood" that he had not
read much of the book ; but over this review in
the *Hour* he was genuinely angry—it hurt him
personally, and, as it afterwards turned out,
played no small part in the story of his life.
The good reviews, however, were many, and
their recommendation of the book hearty ; they
all prophesied that it would be a great success.
Yet, spite of this, "Lynwood's Heritage" didn't
sell. Was it, as I had feared, that Derrick was
too devoid of the pushing faculty ever to make
a successful writer? Or was it that he was
handicapped by being down in the provinces
playing keeper to that abominable old bear?
Anyhow, the book was well received, read with
enthusiasm by an extremely small circle, and
then it dropped down to the bottom among the
mass of overlooked literature, and its career
seemed to be over. I can recall the look in
Derrick's face when one day he glanced through
the new Mudie and Smith lists and found
"Lynwood's Heritage" no longer down. I had
been trying to cheer him up about the book and

quoting all the favourable remarks I had heard
about it.   But unluckily this was damning evidence against my optimist view.

He sighed heavily and put down the lists.

" It's no use to deceive oneself," he said,
drearily, " ' Lynwood ' has failed."

Something in the deep depression of look and
tone gave me a momentary insight into the
author's heart.   He thought, I know, of the
agony of mind this book had cost him; of those
long months of waiting and their deadly struggle,
of the hopes which had made all he passed
through seem so well worth while; and the
bitterness of the disappointment was no doubt
intensified by the knowledge that the Major
would rejoice over it.

We walked that afternoon along the Bradford
Valley, a road which Derrick was specially fond
of.   He loved the thickly-wooded hills, and the
glimpses of the Avon which, flanked by the
canal and the railway, runs parallel with the
high road; he always admired, too, a certain
little village with grey stone cottages which lay
in this direction, and liked to look at the site of
the old hall near the road : nothing remained of

it but the tall gate posts, and rusty iron gates looking strangely dreary and deserted, and within one could see, between some dark yew trees, an old terrace walk with stone steps and balustrades—the most ghostly-looking place you can conceive.

"I know you'll put this into a book some day," I said, laughing.

"Yes," he said, "it is already beginning to simmer in my brain." Apparently his deep disappointment as to his first venture had in no way affected his perfectly clear consciousness that, come what would, he had to write.

As we walked back to Bath he told me his "Ruined Hall" story as far as it had yet evolved itself in his brain, and we were still discussing it when in Milsom Street we met a boy crying evening papers, and details of the last great battle at Saspataras Hill.

Derrick broke off hastily, everything but anxiety for Lawrence driven from his mind.

Chapter VI.

"Say not, O Soul, thou art defeated,
    Because thou art distrest ;
If thou of better things art cheated,
    Thou canst not be of best."—T. T. Lynch.

" Good Heavens, Sydney ! " he exclaimed in great excitement and with his whole face aglow with pleasure, " look here ! "

He pointed to a few lines in the paper which mentioned the heroic conduct of Lieutenant L. Vaughan, who at the risk of his life had rescued a brother officer when surrounded by the enemy and completely disabled. Lieutenant Vaughan had managed to mount the wounded man on his own horse and had miraculously escaped himself with nothing worse than a sword-thrust in the left arm.

We went home in triumph to the Major, and Derrick read the whole account aloud. With all his detestation of war, he was nevertheless

greatly stirred by the description of the gallant
defence of the attacked position—and for a time
we were all at one, and could talk of nothing
but Lawrence's heroism, and Victoria crosses,
and the prospects of peace. However, all too
soon, the Major's fiendish temper returned, and
he began to use the event of the day as a
weapon against Derrick, continually taunting
him with the contrast between his stay-at-home
life of scribbling and Lawrence's life of heroic
adventure. I could never make out whether he
wanted to goad his son into leaving him, in
order that he might drink himself to death in
peace, or whether he merely indulged in his
natural love of tormenting, valuing Derrick's
devotion as conducive to his own comfort, and
knowing that hard words would not drive him
from what he deemed his duty. I rather incline
to the latter view, but the old Major was always
an enigma to me; nor can I to this day make
out his *raison-d'être*, except on the theory that
the training of a novelist required a course of
slow torture, and that the old man was sent into
the world to be a sort of thorn in the flesh to
Derrick.

What with the disappointment about his first book, and the difficulty of writing his second, the fierce craving for Freda's presence, the struggle not to allow his admiration for Lawrence's bravery to become poisoned by envy under the influence of the Major's incessant attacks, Derrick had just then a hard time of it. He never complained, but I noticed a great change in him; his melancholy increased, his flashes of humour and merriment became fewer and fewer—I began to be afraid that he would break down.

"For God's sake!" I exclaimed one evening when left alone with the Doctor after an evening of whist, "do order the Major to London. Derrick has been mewed up here with him for nearly two years, and I don't think he can stand it much longer."

So the Doctor kindly contrived to advise the Major to consult a well-known London physician, and to spend a fortnight in town, further suggesting that a month at Ben Rhydding might be enjoyable before settling down at Bath again for the winter. Luckily the Major took to the idea, and just as Lawrence returned from the war Derrick and his father arrived in town. The change seemed likely to work well, and I was able now and then to release my friend and play cribbage with the old man for an hour or two while Derrick tore about London, interviewed his publisher, made researches into seventeenth century documents at the British Museum, and somehow managed in his rapid way to acquire those glimpses of life and character which he afterwards turned to such good account. All was grist that came to his mill, and at first the mere sight of his old home, London, seemed to revive him. Of course at the very first opportunity he called at the Probyns', and we both of us had an invitation to go there on the following Wednesday to see the march past of the troops and to lunch. Derrick was nearly beside himself at the prospect, for he knew that he should certainly meet Freda at last, and the mingled pain and bliss of being actually in the same place with her, yet as completely separated as if seas rolled between them, was beginning to try him terribly.

Meantime Lawrence had turned up again, greatly improved in every way by all that he had

F

lived through, but rather too ready to fall in with his father's tone towards Derrick. The relations between the two brothers—always a little peculiar—became more and more difficult, and the Major seemed to enjoy pitting them against each other.

At length the day of the review arrived. Derrick was not looking well, his eyes were heavy with sleeplessness, and the Major had been unusually exasperating at breakfast that morning, so that he started with a jaded, worn-out feeling that would not wholly yield even to the excitement of this long-expected meeting with Freda. When he found himself in the great drawing-room at Lord Probyn's house, amid a buzz of talk and a crowd of strange faces, he was seized with one of those sudden attacks of shyness to which he was always liable. In fact, he had been so long alone with the old Major that this plunge into society was too great a reaction, and the very thing he had so longed for became a torture to him.

Freda was at the other end of the room talking to Keith Collins, the well-known member for Codrington, whose curious but attractive face was known to all the world through the caricatures of it in "Punch." I knew that she saw Derrick, and that he instantly perceived her, and that a miserable sense of separation, of distance, of hopelessness overwhelmed him as he looked. After all, it was natural enough. For two years he had thought of Freda night and day; in his unutterably dreary life her memory had been his refreshment, his solace, his companion. Now he was suddenly brought face to face, not with the Freda of his dreams, but with a fashionable, beautifully dressed, much-sought girl, and he felt that a gulf lay between them; it was the gulf of experience. Freda's life in society, the whirl of gaiety, the excitement and success which she had been enjoying throughout the season, and his miserable monotony of companionship with his invalid father, of hard work and weary disappointment, had broken down the bond of union that had once existed between them. From either side they looked at each other—Freda with a wondering perplexity, Derrick with a dull grinding pain at his heart.

Of course they spoke to each other; but I

fancy the merest platitudes passed between them. Somehow they had lost touch, and a crowded London drawing-room was hardly the place to regain it.

"So your novel is really out," I heard her say to him in that deep, clear voice of hers. "I like the design on the cover."

"Oh, have you read the book?" said Derrick, colouring.

"Well, no," she said, truthfully. "I wanted to read it, but my father wouldn't let me—he is very particular about what we read."

That frank but not very happily worded answer was like a stab to poor Derrick. He had given to the world then a book that was not fit for her to read! This "Lynwood," which had been written with his own heart's blood, was counted a dangerous, poisonous thing, from which she must be guarded!

Freda must have seen that she had hurt him, for she tried hard to retrieve her words.

"It was tantalizing to have it actually in the house, wasn't it? I have a grudge against the *Hour*, for it was the review in that which set my father against it." Then, rather anxious to leave the difficult subject—"And has your brother quite recovered from his wound?"

I think she was a little vexed that Derrick did not show more animation in his replies about Lawrence's adventures during the war; the less he responded the more enthusiastic she became, and I am perfectly sure that in her heart she was thinking—

"He is jealous of his brother's fame—I am disappointed in him. He has grown dull, and absent, and stupid, and he is dreadfully wanting in small-talk. I fear that his life down in the provinces is turning him into a bear."

She brought the conversation back to his book; but there was a little touch of scorn in her voice, as if she thought to herself, "I suppose he is one of those people who can only talk on one subject—his own doings." Her manner was almost brusque.

"Your novel has had a great success, has it not?" she asked.

He instantly perceived her thought, and replied with a touch of dignity and a proud smile:

"On the contrary, it has been a great failure;

only three hundred and nine copies have been sold."

"I wonder at that," said Freda, "for one so often hears it talked of."

He promptly changed the topic, and began to speak of the march past. "I .want to see Lord Starcross," he added. "I have no idea what a hero is like."

Just then Lady Probyn came up, followed by an elderly harpy in spectacles and false, much-frizzed fringe.

"Mrs. Carsteen wishes to be introduced to you, Mr. Vaughan; she is a great admirer of your writings."

And poor Derrick, who was then quite unused to the species, had to stand and receive a flood of the most fulsome flattery, delivered in a strident voice, and to bear the critical and prolonged stare of the spectacled eyes. Nor would the harpy easily release her prey. She kept him much against his will, and I saw him looking wistfully now and then towards Freda.

"It amuses me," I said to her, "that Derrick Vaughan should be so anxious to see Lord Starcross. It reminds me of Charles Lamb's anxiety to see Koscuisko, ' for,' said he, ' I have never seen a hero ; I wonder how they look,' while all the time he himself was living a life of heroic self-sacrifice."

"Mr. Vaughan, I should think, need only look at his own brother," said Freda, missing the drift of my speech.

I longed to tell her what it was possible to tell of Derrick's life, but at that moment Sir Richard Merrifield introduced to his daughter a girl in a huge hat and great flopping sleeves, Miss Isaacson, whose picture at the Grosvenor had been so much talked of. Now the little artist knew no one in the room, and Freda saw fit to be extremely friendly to her. She was introduced to me, and I did my best to talk to her and set Freda at liberty as soon as the harpy had released Derrick ; but my endeavours were frustrated, for Miss Isaacson, having looked me well over, decided that I was not at all intense, but a mere commonplace, slightly cynical world-ling, and having exchanged a few lukewarm remarks with me, she returned to Freda, and stuck to her like a bur for the rest of the time.

We stood out on the balcony to see the troops

go by. It was a fine sight, and we all became
highly enthusiastic. Freda enjoyed the mere
pageant like a child, and was delighted with the
horses. She looked now more like the Freda of
the yacht, and I wished that Derrick could be
near her; but, as ill-luck would have it, he was
at some distance, hemmed in by an impassable
barrier of eager spectators.

Lawrence Vaughan rode past, looking wonderfully well in his uniform. He was riding a
spirited bay, which took Freda's fancy amazingly, though she reserved her chief enthusiasm
for Lord Starcross and his steed. It was not
until all was over, and we had returned to the
drawing-room, that Derrick managed to get the
talk with Freda for which I knew he was longing, and then they were fated, apparently, to
disagree. I was standing near and overheard
the close of their talk.

"I do believe you must be a member of the
Peace Society!" said Freda impatiently. "Or
perhaps you have turned Quaker. But I want
to introduce you to my godfather, Mr. Fleming;
you know it was his son whom your brother
saved."

And I heard Derrick being introduced as the brother of the hero of Saspataras Hill ; and the next day he received a card for one of Mrs. Fleming's receptions, Lawrence having previously been invited to dine there on the same night.

What happened at that party I never exactly understood. All I could gather was that Lawrence had been tremendously fêted, that Freda had been present, and that poor old Derrick was as miserable as he could be when I next saw him. Putting two and two together, I guessed that he had been tantalised by a mere sight of her, possibly tortured by watching more favoured men enjoying long *tête-à-têtes ;* but he would say little or nothing about it, and when, soon after, he and the Major left London, I feared that the fortnight had done my friend harm instead of good.

CHAPTER VII.

"'Then in that hour rejoice, since only thus
    Can thy proud heart grow wholly piteous.
    Thus only to the world thy speech can flow
    Charged with the sad authority of woe.
    Since no man nurtured in the shade can sing
    To a true note one psalm of conquering ;
    Warriors must chant it whom our own eyes see
    Red from the battle and more bruised than we,
    Men who have borne the worst, have known the whole,
    Have felt the last abeyance of the soul."
                                    F. W. H. MYERS.

ABOUT the beginning of August, I rejoined him
at Ben Rhydding. The place suited the Major
admirably, and his various baths took up so
great a part of each day, that Derrick had more
time to himself than usual, and "At Strife" got
on rapidly. He much enjoyed too the beautiful
country round, while the hotel itself, with its
huge gathering of all sorts and conditions of
people, afforded him endless studies of character. The Major breakfasted in his own room,

and, being so much engrossed with his baths,
did not generally appear till twelve. Derrick
and I breakfasted in the great dining-hall ; and
one morning, when the meal was over, we, as
usual, strolled into the drawing-room to see if
there were any letters awaiting us.

"One for you," I remarked, handing him a
thick envelope.

" From Lawrence ! " he exclaimed.

" Well, don't read it in here ; the Doctor will be
coming to read prayers. Come out in the
garden," I said.

We went out into the beautiful grounds, and
he tore open the envelope and began to read his
letter as we walked. All at once I felt the arm
which was linked in mine give a quick involun-
tary movement, and, looking up, saw that Derrick
had turned deadly pale.

"What's up ? " I said. But he read on without replying ; and, when I paused and sat down
on a sheltered rustic seat, he unconsciously
followed my example, looking more like a sleep-
walker than a man in the possession of all his
faculties. At last he finished the letter, and
looked up in a dazed, miserable way, letting his

eyes wander over the fir-trees and the fragrant shrubs and the flowers by the path.

"Dear old fellow, what is the matter?" I asked.

The words seemed to rouse him.

A dreadful look passed over his face—the look of one stricken to the heart. But his voice was perfectly calm, and full of a ghastly self-control.

"Freda will be my sister-in-law," he said, rather as if stating the fact to himself than answering my question.

"Impossible!" I said. "What do you mean? How could——"

As if to silence me he thrust the letter into my hand. It ran as follows:—

" DEAR DERRICK,—For the last few days I have been down at the Flemings' place in Derbyshire, and fortune has favoured me, for the Merrifields are here too. Now prepare yourself for a surprise. Break the news to the governor, ánd send me your heartiest congratulations by return of post. I am engaged to Freda Merrifield, and am the happiest fellow in the world. They are awfully fastidious sort of people, and I do not believe Sir Richard would have consented to such a match had it not been for that lucky impulse which made me rescue Dick Fleming. It has all been arranged very quickly, as these things should be, but we have seen a good deal of each other— first at Aldershot the year before last, and just lately in town, and now these four days down here—and days in a country house are equal to weeks elsewhere. I enclose a letter to my father—give it to him at a suitable moment— but, after all, he's sure to approve of a daughter-in-law with such a dowry as Miss Merrifield is likely to have.

"Yours affly.,

"LAWRENCE VAUGHAN."

I gave him back the letter without a word. In dead silence we moved on, took a turning which led to a little narrow gate, and passed out of the grounds to the wild moorland country be- yond.

After all, Freda was in no way to blame. As a mere girl she had allowed Derrick to see that she cared for him ; then circumstances had en- tirely separated them ; she saw more of the world, met Lawrence, was perhaps first attracted to him by his very likeness to Derrick, and finally fell in love with the hero of the season, whom every one delighted to honour. Nor could one blame Lawrence, who had no notion that he had supplanted his brother. All the blame lay with the Major's slavery to drink, for if only he had remained out in India I feel sure that matters would have gone quite differently.

We tramped on over heather and ling and

springy turf till we reached the old ruin known
as the Hunting Tower ; then Derrick seemed to
awake to the recollection of present things.   He
looked at his watch.

"I must go back to my father," he said, for the
first time breaking the silence.

"You shall do no such thing!" I cried.
"Stay out here, and I will see to the Major, and
give him the letter too if you like."

He caught at the suggestion, and as he
thanked me I think there were tears in his eyes.
So I took the letter and set off for Ben Rhydding, leaving him to get what relief he could
from solitude, space, and absolute quiet.   Once
I just glanced back, and somehow the scene has
always lingered in my memory—the great
stretch of desolate moor, the dull crimson of the
heather, the lowering gray clouds, the Hunting
Tower a patch of deeper gloom against the
gloomy sky, and Derrick's figure prostrate on
the turf, the face hidden, the hands grasping at
the sprigs of heather growing near.

The Major was just ready to be helped into
the garden when I reached the hotel.   We sat
down in the very same place where Derrick had

read the news, and, when I judged it politic, I
suddenly remembered with apologies the letter
that had been intrusted to me. The old man
received it with satisfaction, for he was fond of
Lawrence and proud of him, and the news of the
engagement pleased him greatly. He was still
discussing it when, two hours later, Derrick returned.

"Here's good news!" said the Major, glancing
up as his son approached. "Trust Lawrence to
fall on his feet! He tells me the girl will have
a thousand a year. You know her, don't you?
What's she like?"

"I have met her," replied Derrick, with forced
composure. "She is very charming."

"Lawrence has all his wits about him," growled
the Major. "Whereas you——" (several oaths
interjected). "It will be a long while before
any girl with a dowry will look at you! What
women like is a bold man of action ; what they
despise, mere dabblers in pen and ink, writers of
poisonous sensational tales such as yours! I'm
quoting your own reviewers, so you needn't con-
tradict me!"

Of course no one had dreamt of contradicting; it would have been the worst possible policy.

"Shall I help you in?" said Derrick. "It is just dinner time."

And as I walked beside them to the hotel, listening to the Major's flood of irritating words, and glancing now and then at Derrick's grave resolute face, which successfully masked such bitter suffering, I couldn't help reflecting that here was courage infinitely more deserving of the Victoria Cross than Lawrence's impulsive rescue. Very patiently he sat through the long dinner. I doubt if any but an acute observer could have told that he was in trouble; and, luckily, the world in general observes hardly at all. He endured the Major till it was time for him to take a Turkish bath, and then, having two hours' freedom, climbed with me up the rock-covered hill at the back of the hotel. He was very silent. But I remember that, as we watched the sun go down—a glowing crimson ball, half veiled in gray mist—he said abruptly, "If Lawrence makes her happy I can bear it. And of course I always knew that I was not worthy of her."

Derrick's room was a large, gaunt, ghostly

place in one of the towers of the hotel, and in
one corner of it was a winding stair leading to
the roof. When I went in next morning I found
him writing away at his novel just as usual, but
when I looked at him it seemed to me that the
night had aged him fearfully. As a rule, he took
interruptions as a matter of course, and with
perfect sweetness of temper; but to-day he
seemed unable to drag himself back to the outer
world. He was writing at a desperate pace too,
and frowned when I spoke to him. I took up
the sheet of foolscap which he had just finished
and glanced at the number of the page—evidently he had written an immense quantity since
the previous day.

"You will knock yourself up if you go on at
this rate!" I exclaimed.

"Nonsense!" he said sharply. "You know
it never tires me."

Yet, all the same, he passed his hand very
wearily over his forehead, and stretched himself
with the air of one who had been in a cramping
position for many hours.

"You have broken your vow!" I cried. "You
have been writing at night."

G

"No," he said; "it was morning when
I began—three o'clock. And it pays better
to get up and write than to lie awake thinking."

Judging by the speed with which the novel
grew in the next few weeks, I could tell that
Derrick's nights were of the worst.

He began, too, to look very thin and haggard,
and I more than once noticed that curious
"sleep-walking" expression in his eyes; he
seemed to me just like a man who has received
his death-blow, yet still lingers—half alive, half
dead. I had an odd feeling that it was his
novel which kept him going, and I began to
wonder what would happen when it was finished.

A month later, when I met him again at Bath
he had written the last chapter of "At Strife,"
and we read it over the sitting-room fire on the
Saturday evening. I was very much struck
with the book; it seemed to me a great advance
on "Lynwood's Heritage," and the part which
he had written since that day at Ben Rhydding
was full of an indescribable power, as if the life
of which he had been robbed had flowed into
his work. When he had done, he tied up the

MS. in his usual prosaic fashion, just as if it had been a bundle of clothes, and put it on a side table.

It was arranged that I should take it to Davison—the publisher of " Lynwood's Heritage "—on Monday, and see what offer he would make for it. Just at that time I felt so sorry for Derrick that if he had asked me to hawk round fifty novels I would have done it.

Sunday morning proved wet and dismal ; as a rule the Major, who was fond of music, attended service at the Abbey, but the weather forced him now to stay at home. I myself was at that time no church-goer, but Derrick would, I verily believe, as soon have fasted a week as have given up a Sunday morning service; and having no mind to be left to the Major's company, and a sort of wish to be near my friend, I went with him. I believe it is not correct to admire Bath Abbey, but for all that "the lantern of the west" has always seemed to me a grand place ; as for Derrick, he had a horror of a "dim religious light," and always stuck up for its huge windows, and I believe he loved the Abbey with all his heart. Indeed, taking it only from a sensuous point of view, I could quite imagine what a re-

lief he found his weekly attendance here ; by contrast with his home the place was Heaven itself.

As we walked back, I asked a question that
had long been in my mind ; " Have you seen
anything of Lawrence ? "

" He saw us across London on our way from Ben
Rhydding," said Derrick, steadily. "Freda came
with him, and my father was delighted with her."

I wondered how they had got through the
meeting, but of course my curiosity had to go
unsatisfied. Of one thing I might be certain,
namely, that Derrick had gone through with it
like a Trojan, that he had smiled and congratu-
lated in his quiet way, and had done his best to
efface himself and think only of Freda. But as
everyone knows—

> " Face joy's a costly mask to wear,
> 'Tis bought with pangs long nourishèd
> And rounded to despair; "

and he looked now even more worn and old
than he had done at Ben Rhydding in the first
days of his trouble.

However, he turned resolutely away from the
subject I had introduced and began to discuss
titles for his novel.

"It's impossible to find anything new," he said, "absolutely impossible. I declare I shall take to numbers."

I laughed at this prosaic notion, and we were still discussing the title when we reached home.

"Don't say anything about it at lunch," he said as we entered. "My father detests my writing."

I nodded assent and opened the sitting-room door—a strong smell of brandy instantly became apparent; the Major sat in the green velvet chair, which had been wheeled close to the hearth. He was drunk.

Derrick gave an ejaculation of utter hopelessness.

"This will undo all the good of Ben Rhydding!" he said. "How on earth has he managed to get it?"

The Major, however, was not so far gone as he looked; he caught up the remark and turned towards us with a hideous laugh.

"Ah, yes," he said, "that's the question. But the old man has still some brains, you see. I'll be even with you yet, Derrick. You needn't think you're to have it all your own way. It's my turn now. You've deprived me all this time of the only thing I care for in life, and now I turn the tables on you. Tit for tat. Oh! yes, I've turned your d——d scribblings to a useful purpose, so you needn't complain!"

All this had been shouted out at the top of his voice and freely interlarded with expressions which I will not repeat; at the end he broke again into a laugh, and with a look, half idiotic, half devilish, pointed towards the grate.

"Good Heavens!" I said, "what have you done?"

By the side of the chair I saw a piece of brown paper, and, catching it up, read the address—"Messrs. Davison, Paternoster Row"—in the fireplace was a huge charred mass. Derrick caught his breath; he stooped down and snatched from the fender a fragment of paper slightly burned, but still not charred beyond recognition like the rest. The writing was quite legible—it was his own writing—the description of the Royalist's attack, and Paul Wharncliffe's defence of the bridge. I looked from the half-burnt scrap of paper to the side table where, only the previous night, we had placed the novel, and then, realising as far as any but

an author could realise, the frightful thing that
had happened, I looked in Derrick's face. It's
white fury appalled me. What he had borne
hitherto from the Major, God only knows, but
this was the last drop in the cup. Daily insults,
ceaseless provocation, even the humiliation of
personal violence he had borne with superhuman
patience; but this last injury, this wantonly
cruel outrage, this deliberate destruction of an
amount of thought, and labour, and suffering
which only the writer himself could fully estimate—this was intolerable.

What might have happened had the Major
been sober and in the possession of ordinary
physical strength I hardly care to think. As it
was, his weakness protected him. Derrick's
wrath was speechless; with one look of loathing
and contempt at the drunken man, he strode
out of the room, caught up his hat, and hurried
from the house.

The Major sat chuckling to himself for a
minute or two, but soon he grew drowsy, and
before long was snoring like a grampus. The
old landlady brought in lunch, saw the state of
things pretty quickly, shook her head and com-

miserated Derrick. Then, when she had left the room, seeing no prospect that either of my companions would be in a fit state for lunch, I made a solitary meal, and had just finished when a cab stopped at the door, and out sprang Derrick. I went into the passage to meet him.

"The Major is asleep," I remarked.

He took no more notice than if I had spoken of the cat.

"I'm going to London," he said, making for the stairs. "Can you get your bag ready? There's a train at 2·5."

Somehow the suddenness and the self-control with which he made this announcement carried me back to the hotel at Southampton, where, after listening to the account of the ship's doctor, he had announced his intention of living with his father. For more than two years he had borne this awful life ; he had lost pretty nearly all that there was to be lost, and he had gained the Major's vindictive hatred. Now, half maddened by pain and having, as he thought, so hopelessly failed, he saw nothing for it but to go—and that at once.

I packed my bag, and then went to help him.

He was cramming all his possessions into port-
manteaux and boxes; the Hoffman was already
packed, and the wall looked curiously bare without it.   Clearly this was no visit to London—he
was leaving Bath for good, and who could
wonder at it ?

"I have arranged for the attendant from the
hospital to come in at night as well as in the
morning," he said, as he locked a portmanteau
that was stuffed almost to bursting.   "What's
the time ? We must make haste or we shall
lose the train.   Do, like a good fellow, cram
that heap of things into the carpet-bag while I
speak to the landlady."

At last we were off, rattling through the quiet
streets of Bath, and reaching the station barely
in time to rush up the long flight of stairs and
spring into an empty carriage.   Never shall I
forget that journey.   The train stopped at every
single station, and sometimes in between ; we
were five mortal hours on the road, and more
than once I thought Derrick would have fainted.
However, he was not of the fainting order, he
only grew more and more ghastly in colour and
rigid in expression.

I felt very anxious about him, for the shock and the sudden anger following on the trouble about Freda seemed to me enough to unhinge even a less sensitive nature. "At Strife" was the novel which had, I firmly believe, kept him alive through that awful time at Ben Rhydding, and I began to fear that the Major's fit of drunken malice might prove the destruction of the author as well as of the book. Everything had, as it were, come at once on poor Derrick ; yet I don't know that he fared worse than other people in this respect.

Life, unfortunately, is for most of us no well-arranged story with a happy termination ; it is a chequered affair of shade and sun, and for one beam of light there come very often wide patches of shadow. Men seem to have known this so far back as Shakespeare's time, and to have observed that one woe trod on another's heels, to have battled not with a single wave, but with a "sea of troubles," and to have remarked that "sorrows come not singly, but in battalions."

However, owing I believe chiefly to his own self-command, and to his untiring faculty for taking infinite pains over his work, Derrick did

not break down, but pleasantly cheated my expectations.   I was not called on to nurse him
through a fever, and consumption did not mark
him for her own.   In fact, in the matter of illness, he was always a most prosaic, unromantic
fellow, and never indulged in any of the euphoni-
ous and interesting ailments.   In all his life, I
believe, he never went in for anything but the
mumps—of all complaints the least interesting
—and, may be, an occasional headache.

However, all this is a digression.   We at
length reached London, and Derrick took a
room above mine, now and then disturbing me
with nocturnal pacings over the creaking boards,
but, on the whole, proving himself the best of
companions.

If I wrote till Doomsday, I could never make
you understand how the burning of his novel
affected him—to this day it is a subject I in-
stinctively avoid with him—though the re-
written "At Strife" has been such a grand
success.   For he did re-write the story, and that
at once.   He said little ; but the very next
morning, in one of the windows of our quiet
sitting-room, often enough looking out despair-

ingly at the grey monotony of Montague Street, he began at "Page 1, Chapter 1," and so worked patiently on for many months to re-make as far as he could what his drunken father had maliciously destroyed. Beyond the unburnt paragraph about the attack on Mondisfield, he had nothing except a few hastily-scribbled ideas in his note-book, and of course the very elaborate and careful historical notes which he had made on the Civil War during many years of reading and research—for this period had always been a favourite study with him.

But, as any author will understand, the effort of re-writing was immense, and this, combined with all the other troubles, tried Derrick to the utmost. However, he toiled on, and I have always thought that his resolute, unyielding conduct with regard to that book proved what a man he was.

CHAPTER VIII.

"How oft Fate's sharpest blow shall leave thee strong,
With some re-risen ecstacy of song."

F. W. H. MYERS.

As the autumn wore on, we heard now and then
from old Mackrill the doctor. His reports of
the Major were pretty uniform. Derrick used
to hand them over to me when he had read
them ; but, by tacit consent, the Major's name
was never mentioned.

Meantime, besides re-writing "At Strife," he
was accumulating material for his next book
and working to very good purpose. Not a
minute of his day was idle ; he read much, saw
various phases of life hitherto unknown to him,
studied, observed, gained experience, and contrived, I believe, to think very little and very
guardedly of Freda.

But, on Christmas Eve, I noticed a change in
him—and that very night he spoke to me. For

such an impressionable fellow, he had really extraordinary tenacity, and, spite of the course of Herbert Spencer that I had put him through, he retained his unshaken faith in many things which to me were at that time the merest legends. I remember very well the arguments we used to have on the vexed question of "Free-will," and being myself more or less of a fatalist, it annoyed me that I never could in the very slightest degree shake his convictions on that point. Moreover, when I plagued him too much with Herbert Spencer, he had a way of retaliating, and would foist upon me his favourite authors. He was never a worshipper of any one writer, but always had at least a dozen prophets in whose praise he was enthusiastic.

Well, on this Christmas Eve, we had been to see dear old Ravenscroft and his grand-daughter, and we were walking back through the quiet precincts of the Temple, when he said abruptly—

"I have decided to go back to Bath, to-morrow."

" Have you had a worse account ? " I asked, much startled at this sudden announcement.

" No ; " he replied, " but the one I had a week

ago was far from good if you remember, and I
have a feeling that I ought to be there."

At that moment we emerged into the con-
fusion of Fleet Street; but when we had
crossed the road I began to remonstrate with
him, and argued the folly of the idea all the way
down Chancery Lane.

However, there was no shaking his purpose;
Christmas and its associations had made his life
in town no longer possible for him.

"I must at any rate try it again and see how
it works," he said.

And all I could do was to persuade him to
leave the bulk of his possessions in London, "in
case," as he remarked, "the Major would not
have him."

So the next day I was left to myself again
with nothing to remind me of Derrick's stay but
his pictures which still hung on the wall of our
sitting-room.   I made him promise to write a
full, true, and particular account of his return, a
bonâ fide old-fashioned letter, not the half-dozen
lines of these degenerate days; and about a week
later I received the following budget—

"DEAR SYDNEY,—

"I got down to Bath all right, and, thanks
to your 'Study of sociology,' endured a slow and cold and
dull and depressing journey with the thermometer down
to zero, and spirits to correspond, with the country a
monotonous white, and the sky a monotonous grey, and
a companion who smoked the vilest tobacco you can
conceive. The old place looks as beautiful as ever, and
to my great satisfaction the hills round about are green.
Snow, save in pictures, is an abomination. Milsom Street
looked asleep, and Gay Street decidedly dreary, but the
inhabitants were roused by my knock, and the old landlady nearly shook my hand off. My father has an attack
of jaundice and is in a miserable state. He was asleep
when I got here, and the good old landlady, thinking the
front sitting-room would be free, had invited 'company,'
i.e., two or three married daughters and their belongings ;
one of the children beats Magnay's 'Carina' as to beauty
—he ought to paint her. Happy thought, send him and
pretty Mrs. Espérance down here on spec. He can
paint the child for the next Academy, and meantime I
could enjoy his company. Well, all these good folks
being just set-to at roast beef, I naturally wouldn't hear
of disturbing them, and in the end was obliged to sit
down too, and eat at that hour of the day the hugest
dinner you ever saw—anything but voracious appetites
offended the hostess. Magnay's future model, for all its
angelic face, 'ate to repletion' like the fair American in
the story. Then I went into my father's room, and
shortly after he woke up and asked me to give him some
Friedrichshall water, making no comment at all on my
return, but just behaving as though I had been here all
the autumn, so that I felt as if the whole affair were a
dream. Except for this attack of jaundice, he has been
much as usual, and when you next come down you will

find us settled into our old groove. The quiet of it after London is extraordinary. But I believe it suits the book, which gets on pretty fast. This afternoon I went up Lansdowne and right on past the Grand Stand to Prospect Stile, which is at the edge of a high bit of table-land, and looks over a splendid stretch of country, with the Bristol Channel and the Welsh hills in the distance. While I was there the sun most considerately set in gorgeous array. You never saw anything like it. It was worth the journey from London to Bath, I can assure you. Tell Magnay, and may it lure him down ; also name the model aforementioned.

"How is the old Q.C. and his pretty grandchild? That quaint old room of theirs in the Temple somehow took my fancy, and the child was divine. Do you re-member my showing you, in a gloomy narrow street here, a jolly old watchmaker who sits in his shop-window and is for ever bending over sick clocks and watches ? Well, he's still sitting there, as if he had never moved since we saw him that Saturday months ago. I mean to study him for a portrait ; his sallow, clean-shaved, wrinkled face has a whole story in it. I believe he is married to a Xanthippe who throws cold water over him, both literally and metaphorically ; but he is a philosopher—I'll stake my reputation as an observer on that—he just shrugs his sturdy old shoulders, and goes on mending clocks and watches. On dark days he works by a gas jet—and then Rembrandt would enjoy painting him. I look at him whenever my world is particularly awry, and find him highly beneficial. Davison has forwarded me to-day two letters from readers of 'Lynwood.' The first is from an irate female who takes me to task for the dangerous tendency of the story, and insists that I have drawn impossible circumstances and impossible characters.

H

The second is from an old clergyman, who writes a pathetic letter of thanks, and tells me that it is almost word for word the story of a son of his who died five years ago. Query : shall I send the irate female the old man's letter, and save myself the trouble of writing? But on the whole I think not, it would be pearls before swine. I will write to her myself.   Glad to see you whenever you can run down.

" Yours ever,

"D. V."

" (Never struck me before what pious initials mine are)."

The very evening I received this letter, I happened to be dining at the Probyn's.   As luck would have it, pretty Miss Freda was stay-ing in the house, and she fell to my share.   I always liked her, though of late I had felt rather angry with her for being carried away by the general storm of admiration and swept by it into an engagement with Lawrence Vaughan.   She was a very pleasant, natural sort of talker, and she always treated me as an old friend.   But she seemed to me, that night, a little less satisfied than usual with life.   Perhaps it was merely the effect of the black lace dress which she wore, but I fancied her paler and thinner, and some-how she seemed all eyes.

"Where is Lawrence now?" I asked, as we went down to the dining-room.

" He is stationed at Dover," she replied. " He
was up here for a few hours yesterday ; he came
to say good-bye to me, for I am going to Bath
next Monday with my father, who has been
very rheumatic lately—and you know Bath is
coming into fashion again, all the doctors recom-
mend it."

" Major Vaughan is there," I said, " and has
found the waters very good, I believe ; any day,
at twelve o'clock, you may see him getting out
of his chair and going into the Pump Room on
Derrick's arm. I often wonder what outsiders
think of them. It isn't often, is it, that one sees
a son absolutely giving up his life to his invalid
father ? "

She looked a little startled.

" I wish Lawrence could be more with Major
Vaughan," she said ; " for he is his father's
favourite. You see he is such a good talker,
and Derrick—well, he is absorbed in his books ;
and then he has such extravagant notions about
war, he must be a very uncongenial companion
to the poor Major."

I devoured turbot in wrathful silence. Freda
glanced at me.

"It is true, isn't it, that he has quite given up his life to writing, and cares for nothing else?"

"Well, he has deliberately sacrificed his best chance of success by leaving London and burying himself in the provinces," I replied drily; "and as to caring for nothing but writing, why he never gets more than two or three hours a day for it." And then I gave her a minute account of his daily routine.

She began to look troubled.

"I have been misled," she said; "I had gained quite a wrong impression of him."

"Very few people know anything at all about him," I said warmly; "you are not alone in that."

"I suppose his next novel is finished now?" said Freda; "he told me he had only one or two more chapters to write when I saw him a few months ago on his way from Ben Rhydding. What is he writing now?"

"He is writing that novel over again," I replied.

"Over again? What fearful waste of time!"

"Yes, it has cost him hundreds of hours' work;

it just shows what a man he is that he has gone
through with it so bravely."

"But how do you mean? Didn't it do?"

Rashly, perhaps, yet I think unavoidably, I
told her the truth.

"It was the best thing he had ever written,
but unfortunately it was destroyed, burnt to a
cinder.   That was not very pleasant, was it, for
a man who never makes two copies of his work?".

"It was frightful!" said Freda, her eyes
dilating. "I never heard a word about it.
Does Lawrence know?"

"No, he does not; and perhaps I ought not
to have told you, but I was annoyed at your so
misunderstanding Derrick.   Pray never mention
the affair, he would wish it kept perfectly quiet."

"Why?" asked Freda, turning her clear eyes
full upon mine.

"Because," I said, lowering my voice, "because
his father burnt it."

She almost gasped.

"Deliberately?"

"Yes, deliberately," I replied.   "His illness
has affected his temper, and he is sometimes
hardly responsible for his actions."

"Oh, I knew that he was irritable and hasty, and that Derrick annoyed him. Lawrence told me that, long ago," said Freda. "But that he should have done such a thing as that! It is horrible! Poor Derrick, how sorry I am for him. I hope we shall see something of them at Bath. Do you know how the Major is?"

"I had a letter about him from Derrick only this evening," I replied, "if you care to see it, I will show it you later on."

And by-and-by, in the drawing-room, I put Derrick's letter into her hands, and explained to her how for a few months he had given up his life at Bath, in despair, but now had returned.

"I don't think Lawrence can understand the state of things," she said wistfully. "And yet he has been down there."

I made no reply, and Freda, with a sigh, turned away.

A month later I went down to Bath and found, as my friend foretold, everything going on in the old groove, except that Derrick himself had an odd, strained look about him, as if he were fighting a foe beyond his strength. Freda's arrival at Bath had been very hard on him, it was almost

more than he could endure.   Sir Richard, blind
as a bat, of course, to anything below the surface,
made a point of seeing something of Lawrence's
brother.   And on the day of my arrival Derrick
and I had hardly set out for a walk when we
ran across the old man.

Sir Richard, though rheumatic in the wrists,
was nimble of foot and an inveterate walker.
He was going with his daughter to see over
Beckford's Tower, and invited us to accompany
him.   Derrick, much against the grain, I fancy,
had to talk to Freda, who, in her winter furs
and close-fitting velvet hat, looked more fascinating than ever, while the old man descanted to me
on Bath waters, antiquities, etc., in a long-winded
way that lasted all up the hill.   We made our way
into the cemetery and mounted the tower stairs,
thinking of the past when this dreary place had
been so gorgeously furnished.   Here Derrick
contrived to get ahead with Sir Richard, and
Freda lingered in a sort of alcove with me.

"I have been so wanting to see you," she said,
in an agitated voice.   "Oh, Mr. Wharncliffe, is
it true what I have heard about the Major?
Does he drink?"

" Who told you ? " I said, a little embarrassed.

" It was our landlady," said Freda ; " she is the daughter of the Major's landlady. And you should hear what she says of Derrick ! Why, he must be a downright hero ! All the time I have been half despising him "—she choked back a sob—" he has been trying to save his father from what was certain death to him—so they told me. Do you think it is true ? "

" I know it is," I replied gravely.

" And about his arm—was that true ? "

I signed an assent.

Her grey eyes grew moist.

" Oh," she cried, " how I have been deceived, and how little Lawrence appreciates him ! I think he must know that I've misjudged him, for he seems so odd and shy, and I don't think he likes to talk to me."

I looked searchingly into her truthful grey eyes, thinking of poor Derrick's unlucky love-story.

" You do not understand him," I said ; " and perhaps it is best so."

But the words and the look were rash, for all at once the colour flooded her face. She turned

quickly away, conscious at last that the midsummer dream of those yachting days had to
Derrick been no dream at all, but a life-long
reality.

I felt very sorry for Freda, for she was not at
all the sort of girl who would glory in having a
fellow hopelessly in love with her.   I knew that
the discovery she had made would be nothing
but a sorrow to her, and could guess how she
would reproach herself for that innocent past
fancy, which, till now, had seemed to her so
faint and far-away—almost as something belong-
ing to another life.   All at once we heard the
others descending, and she turned to me with
such a frightened, appealing look, that I could
not possibly have helped going to the rescue.   I
plunged abruptly into a discourse on Beckford,
and told her how he used to keep diamonds in a
tea-cup, and amused himself by arranging them
on a piece of velvet.   Sir Richard fled from the
sound of my prosy voice, and, needless to say,
Derrick followed him.   We let them get well in
advance and then followed, Freda silent and
distraite, but every now and then asking a question about the Major.

As for Derrick, evidently he was on guard. He saw a good deal of the Merrifields and was sedulously attentive to them in many small ways ; but with Freda he was curiously reserved, and if by chance they did talk together, he took good care to bring Lawrence's name into the conversation. On the whole, I believe loyalty was his strongest characteristic, and want of loyalty in others tried him more severely than anything in the world.

As the spring wore on, it became evident to everyone that the Major could not last long. His son's watchfulness and the enforced temperance which the doctors insisted on had prolonged his life to a certain extent, but gradually his sufferings increased and his strength diminished. At last he kept his bed altogether.

What Derrick bore at this time no one can ever know. When, one bright sunshiny Saturday, I went down to see how he was getting on, I found him worn and haggard, too evidently paying the penalty of sleepless nights and thankless care. I was a little shocked to hear that Lawrence had been summoned, but when I was taken into the sick room I realised that they had done wisely to send for the favourite son.

The Major was evidently dying.

Never can I forget the cruelty and malevolence with which his bloodshot eyes rested on Derrick, or the patience with which the dear old fellow bore his father's scathing sarcasms. It was while I was sitting by the bed that the landlady entered with a telegram, which she put into Derrick's hand.

"From Lawrence!" said the dying man triumphantly, "to say by what train we may expect him. Well?" as Derrick still read the message to himself; "can't you speak, you d——d idiot? Have you lost your d——d tongue? What does he say?"

"I am afraid he cannot be here just yet," said Derrick, trying to tone down the curt message; "it seems he cannot get leave."

"Not get leave to see his dying father? What confounded nonsense. Give me the thing here;" and he snatched the telegram from Derrick and read it in a quavering, hoarse voice,

"Impossible to get away. Am hopelessly tied here. Love to my father. Greatly regret to hear such bad news of him."

I think that message made the old man realise the worth of Lawrence's often expressed affection for him.   Clearly it was a great blow to him.   He threw down the paper without a word and closed his eyes.   For half an hour he lay like that, and we did not disturb him.   At last he looked up; his voice was fainter and his manner more gentle.

"Derrick," he said, "I believe I've done you an injustice; it is you who care for me, not Lawrence, and I've struck your name out of my will—have left all to him.   After all, though you are one of those confounded novelists, you've done what you could for me.   Let some one fetch a solicitor—I'll alter it—I'll alter it!"

I instantly hurried out to fetch a lawyer, but it was Saturday afternoon, the offices were closed, and some time passed before I had caught my man.   I told him as we hastened back some of the facts of the case, and he brought his writing materials into the sick room and took down from the Major's own lips the words which would have the effect of dividing the old man's possessions between his two sons. Dr. Mackrill was now present; he stood on one side of the bed, his fingers on the dying man's pulse.   On the other side stood Derrick, a degree paler and graver than usual, but revealing little of his real feelings.

"Word it as briefly as you can," said the doctor.

And the lawyer scribbled away as though for his life, while the rest of us waited in a wretched hushed state of tension.   In the room itself there was no sound save the scratching of the pen and the laboured breathing of the old man; but in the next house we could hear someone playing a waltz.   Somehow it did not seem to me incongruous, for it was " Sweethearts," and that had been the favourite waltz at Ben Rhydding, so that I always connected it with Derrick and his trouble, and now the words rang in my ears—

> " Oh, love for a year, a week, a day,
> But alas ! for the love that loves alway."

If it had not been for the Major's return from India, I firmly believed that Derrick and Freda would by this time have been betrothed.   Derrick had taken a line which necessarily divided

them, had done what he saw to be his duty ;
yet what were the results ?   He had lost Freda,
he had lost his book, he had damaged his chance
of success as a writer, he had been struck out of
his father's will, and he had suffered unspeak-
ably.   Had anything whatever been gained ?
The Major was dying unrepentant to all appearance, as hard and cynical an old worldling
as I ever saw.   The only spark of grace he
showed was that tardy endeavour to make a
fresh will.   What good had it all been ?   What
good ?

I could not answer the question then, could
only cry out in a sort of indignation, "What
profit is there in his blood ?"   But looking at it
now, I have a sort of perception that the very
lack of apparent profitableness was part of
Derrick's training, while if, as I now incline to
think, there is a hereafter where the training
begun here is continued, the old Major in the
hell he most richly deserved would have the
remembrance of his son's patience and con-
stancy and devotion to serve as a guiding light
in the outer darkness.

The lawyer no longer wrote at railroad speed;

he pushed back his chair, brought the will to the bed, and placed the pen in the trembling yellow hand of the invalid.

"You must sign your name here," he said, pointing with his finger ; and the Major raised himself a little, and brought the pen quaver· ingly down towards the paper. With a sort of fascination I watched the finely-pointed. steel nib ; it trembled for an instant or two, then the pen dropped from the convulsed fingers, and with a cry of intolerable anguish the Major fell back.

For some minutes there was a painful struggle ; presently we caught a word or two between the groans of the dying man.

" Too late ! " he gasped, " too late ! " And then a dreadful vision of horrors seemed to rise before him, and with a terror that I can never forget he turned to his son and clutched fast hold of his hands : " Derrick ! " he shrieked.

Derrick could not speak, but he bent low over the bed as though to screen the dying eyes from those horrible visions, and with an odd sort of thrill I saw him embrace his father.

When he raised his head the terror had died out of the Major's face ; all was over.

Chapter IX.

"To duty firm, to conscience true,
  However tried and pressed,
In God's clear sight high work we do,
  If we but do our best."
                                    W. Gaskell.

Lawrence came down to the funeral, and I took good care that he should hear all about his father's last hours, and I made the solicitor show him the unsigned will. He made hardly any comment on it till we three were alone together. Then with a sort of kindly patronage he turned to his brother—Derrick, it must be remembered, was the elder twin—and said pityingly, "Poor old fellow! it was rather rough on you that the governor couldn't sign this; but never mind, you'll soon, no doubt, be earning a fortune by your books; and besides, what does a bachelor want with more than you've already inherited from our mother? Whereas, an officer just going to be married, and with this confounded reputation of hero to keep up, why, I can tell you he needs every penny of it."

Derrick looked at his brother searchingly. I honestly believe that he didn't very much care about the money, but it cut him to the heart that Lawrence should treat him so shabbily. The soul of generosity himself, he could not understand how anyone could frame a speech so infernally mean.

"Of course," I broke in, "if Derrick liked to go to law he could no doubt get his rights; there are three witnesses who can prove what was the Major's real wish."

"I shall not go to law," said Derrick, with a dignity of which I had hardly imagined him capable. "You spoke of your marriage, Lawrence; is it to be soon?'

"This autumn, I hope," said Lawrence; "at least, if I can overcome Sir Richard's ridiculous notion that a girl ought not to marry till she's twenty-one. He's a most crotchetty old fellow, that future father-in-law of mine."

When Lawrence had first come back from the war I had thought him wonderfully improved, but a long course of spoiling and flattery had

I

done him a world of harm. He liked very much to be lionized, and to see him now posing in drawing-rooms, surrounded by a worshipping throng of women, was enough to sicken any sensible being.

As for Derrick, though he could not be expected to feel his bereavement in the ordinary way, yet his father's death had been a great shock to him. It was arranged that after settling various matters in Bath he should go down to stay with his sister for a time, joining me in Montague Street later on. While he was away at Birmingham, however, an extraordinary change came into my humdrum life, and when he rejoined me a few weeks later, I—selfish brute—was so overwhelmed with the trouble that had befallen me that I thought very little indeed of his affairs. He took this quite as a matter of course, and what I should have done without him I can't conceive. However, this story concerns him and has nothing to do with my extraordinary dilemma, I merely mention it as a fact which brought additional cares into his life. All the time he was doing what could be done to help me he was also going through a most baffling and miserable time among the publishers; for "At Strife," unlike its predecessor, was rejected by Davison and by five other houses. Think of this, you comfortable readers, as you lie back in your easy chairs and leisurely turn the pages of that popular story. The book which represented years of study and long hours of hard work was first burnt to a cinder. It was re-written with what infinite pains·and toil few can understand. It was then six times tied up and carried with anxiety and hope to a publisher's office, only to re-appear six times in Montague Street, an unwelcome visitor, bringing with it depression and disappointment.

Derrick said little, but suffered much. However, nothing daunted him. When it came back from the sixth publisher he took it to a seventh, then returned and wrote away like a Trojan at his third book. The one thing that never failed him was that curious consciousness that he *had* to write; like the prophets of old, the "burden" came to him, and speak it he must.

The seventh publisher wrote a somewhat dubious letter: the book he thought had great

merit, but unluckily people were prejudiced, and
historical novels rarely met with success.   However, he was willing to take the story, and offered
half profits, candidly admitting that he had no
great hopes of a large sale.   Derrick instantly
closed with this offer, proofs came in, the book
appeared, was well received like its predecessor,
fell into the hands of one of the leaders of
Society, and, to the intense surprise of the publisher, proved to be the novel of the year.
Speedily a second edition was called for; then,
after a brief interval, a third edition—this time a
rational one-volume affair ; and the whole lot—
6,000 I believe—went off on the day of publication.   Derrick was amazed ; but he enjoyed his
success very heartily, and I think no one
could say that he had leapt into fame at a
bound.

Having devoured " At Strife," people began
to discover the merits of "Lynwood's Heritage";
the libraries were besieged for it, and a cheap
edition was hastily published, and another and
another, till the book, which at first had been
such a dead failure, rivalled " At Strife."   Truly
an author's career is a curious thing ; and pre-

cisely why the first book failed, and the second succeeded, no one could explain.

It amused me very much to see Derrick turned into a lion—he was so essentially un-lion-like. People were for ever asking him how he worked, and I remember a very pretty girl setting upon him once at a dinner-party with the embarrassing request—

"Now do tell me, Mr. Vaughan, how do you write your stories? I wish you would give me a good receipt for a novel."

Derrick hesitated uneasily for a minute; finally, with a humorous smile, said—

"Well, I can't exactly tell you, because, more or less, novels grow; but if you want a receipt, you might perhaps try after this fashion:—Conceive your hero, add a sprinkling of friends and relatives, flavour with whatever scenery or local colour you please, carefully consider what circumstances are most likely to develop your man into the best he is capable of, allow the whole to simmer in your brain as long as you can, and then serve, while hot, with ink upon white or blue foolscap, according to taste."

The young lady applauded the receipt, but

she sighed a little, and probably relinquished all hope of concocting a novel herself; on the whole, it seemed to involve incessant taking of trouble.

About this time I remember too another little scene, which I enjoyed amazingly. I laugh now when I think of it. I happened to be at a huge evening crush, and, rather to my surprise, came across Lawrence Vaughan. We were talking together, when up came Connington of the Foreign Office. "I say, Vaughan," he said, "Lord Remington wishes to be introduced to you." I watched the old statesman a little curiously as he greeted Lawrence, and listened to his first words : "Very glad to make your acquaintance, Captain Vaughan ; I understand that the author of that grand novel, ' At Strife,' is a brother of yours." And poor Lawrence spent a *mauvais quart d'heure*, inwardly fuming I know at the idea that he, the hero of Saspataras Hill, should be considered merely as " the brother of Vaughan, the novelist."

Fate, or perhaps I should say the effect of his own pernicious actions, did not deal kindly just now with Lawrence. Somehow Freda learnt about that will, and, being no bread-and-

butter miss, content meekly to adore her *fiancé*
and deem him faultless, she "up and spake" on
the subject, and I fancy poor Lawrence must
have had another *mauvais quart d'heure*. It was
not this, however, which led to a final breach
between them ; it was something which Sir
Richard discovered with regard to Lawrence's
life at Dover. The engagement was instantly
broken off, and Freda, I am sure, felt nothing
but relief. She went abroad for some time,
however, and we did not see her till long after
Lawrence had been comfortably married to
£1500 a year and a middle-aged widow who
had long been a hero-worshipper, and who, I am
told, never allowed any visitor to leave the house
without making some allusion to the memorable
battle of Saspataras Hill and her Lawrence's
gallant action.

For the two years following after the Major's
death, Derrick and I, as I mentioned before,
shared the rooms in Montague Street. For me,
owing to the trouble I spoke of, they were years
of maddening suspense and pain ; but what
pleasure I did manage to enjoy came entirely
through the success of my friend's books and

from his companionship. It was odd that from
the care of his father he should immediately
pass on to the care of one who had made such a
disastrous mistake as I had made. But I feel
the less compunction at the thought of the
amount of sympathy I called for at that time,
because I notice that the giving of sympathy is
a necessity for Derrick, and that when the
troubles of other folk do not immediately thrust
themselves into his life he carefully hunts them
up. During these two years he was reading for
the Bar—not that he ever expected to do very
much as a barrister, but he thought it well to
have something to fall back on, and declared
that the drudgery of the reading would do him
good. He was also writing as usual, and he
used to spend two evenings a week at White-
chapel, where he taught one of the classes in
connection with Toynbee Hall, and where he
gained that knowledge of East end life which is
conspicuous in his third book—"Dick Carew."
This, with an ever increasing and often very
burdensome correspondence, brought to him by
his books, and with a fair share of dinners, "At
Homes," and so forth, made his life a full one.

In a quiet sort of way I believe he was happy during this time. But later on, when, my trouble at an end, I had migrated to a house of my own, and he was left alone in the Montague Street rooms, his spirits somehow flagged.

Fame is, after all, a hollow, unsatisfying thing to a man of his nature. He heartily enjoyed his success, he delighted in hearing that his books had given pleasure or had been of use to any one, but no public victory' could in the least make up to him for the loss he had suffered in his private life; indeed, I almost think there were times when his triumphs as an author seemed to him utterly worthless—days of depression when the congratulations of his friends were nothing but a mockery. He had gained a striking success, it is true, but he had lost Freda; he was in the position of the starving man who has received a gift of bon-bons, but so craves for bread that they half sicken him. I used now and then to watch his face when, as often happened, someone said : " What an enviable fellow you are, Vaughan, to get on like this ! " or, " What wouldn't I give to change places with you ! " He would invariably smile and turn the

conversation ; but there was a look in his eyes
at such times that I hated to see—it always
made me think of Mrs. Browning's poem, " The
Mask "—

> " Behind no prison-grate, she said,
>   Which slurs the sunshine half a mile,
>   Live captives so uncomforted
>   As souls behind a smile."

As to the Merrifields, there was no chance of
seeing them, for Sir Richard had gone to India
in some official capacity, and no doubt, as every
one said, they would take good care to marry
Freda out there.   Derrick had not seen her
since that trying February at Bath, long ago.
Yet I fancy she was never out of his thoughts.

And so the years rolled on, and Derrick
worked away steadily, giving his books to the
world, accepting the comforts and discomforts
of an author's life, laughing at the outrageous
reports that were in circulation about him, yet
occasionally, I think, inwardly wincing at them,
and learning from the number of begging letters
which he received, and into which he usually
caused searching inquiry to be made, that there

are in the world a vast number of undeserving poor.

One day I happened to meet Lady Probyn at a garden-party; it was at the same house on Campden Hill where I had once met Freda, and perhaps it was the recollection of this which prompted me to enquire after her.

"She has not been well," said Lady Probyn, "and they are sending her back to England; the climate doesn't suit her. She is to make her home with us for the present, so I am the gainer. Freda has always been my favourite niece. I don't know what it is about her that is so taking; she is not half so pretty as the others."

"But so much more charming," I said. "I wonder she has not married out in India, as every one prophesied."

"And so do I," said her aunt. "However, poor child, no doubt, after having been two years engaged to that very disappointing hero of Saspataras Hill, she will be shy of venturing to trust any one again."

"Do you think that affair ever went very deep?" I ventured to ask. "It seemed to me

that she looked miserable during her engagement, and happy when it was broken off."

"Quite so," said Lady Probyn; "I noticed
the same thing. It was nothing but a mistake.
They were not in the least suited to each other.
By-the-by, I hear that Derrick Vaughan is
married."

"Derrick?" I exclaimed; "oh, no, that is a
mistake. It is merely one of the hundred and
one reports that are for ever being set afloat
about him."

"But I saw it in a paper, I assure you," said
Lady Probyn, by no means convinced.

"Ah, that may very well be; they were hard
up for a paragraph, no doubt, and inserted it.
But, as for Derrick, why, how should he marry?
He has been madly in love with Miss Merrifield
ever since our cruise in the *Aurora.*"

Lady Probyn made an inarticulate exclama-
tion.

"Poor fellow!" she said, after a minute's
thought; "that explains much to me."

She did not explain her rather ambiguous remark, and before long our *tete-à-tete* was interrupted.

Now that my friend was a full-fledged barrister, he and I shared chambers ; and one
morning, about a month after this garden party,
Derrick came in with a face of such radiant
happiness, that I couldn't imagine what good
luck had befallen him.

"What do you think?" he exclaimed ; "here's
an invitation for a cruise in the *Aurora* at the
end of August—to be nearly the same party
that we had years ago," and he threw down the
letter for me to read.

Of course there was a special mention of "my
niece, Miss Merrifield, who has just returned
from India, and is ordered plenty of sea-air." I
could have told that without reading the letter,
for it was written quite clearly in Derrick's face.
He looked ten years younger, and if any of his
adoring readers could have seen the pranks he
was up to that morning in our staid and respectable chambers, I am afraid they would no longer
have spoken of him "with 'bated breath and
whispering humbleness."

As it happened, I, too, was able to leave home
for a fortnight at the end of August ; and so our
party in the *Aurora* really was the same, except

that we were all several years older, and let us
hope wiser, than on the previous occasion. Con-
sidering all that had intervened, I was surprised
that Derrick was not more altered ; as for Freda,
she was decidedly paler than when we first met
her, but, before long, sea-air and happiness
wrought a wonderful transformation in her.

In spite of the pessimists who are for ever
writing books—even writing novels (more shame
to them) to prove that there is no such thing as
happiness in the world, we managed every one
of us heartily to enjoy our cruise. It seemed
indeed true that—

" Green leaves and blossoms, and sunny warm weather,
    And singing and loving all come back together."

Something, at any rate, of the glamour of
those past days came back to us all, I fancy, as
we laughed and dozed and idled and talked be-
neath the snowy wings of the *Aurora*, and I
cannot say I was in the least surprised when, on
roaming through the pleasant garden walks in
that unique little island of Tresco, I came once
more upon Derrick and Freda, with, if you will
believe it, another handful of white heather

given to them by that discerning gardener! Freda once more reminded me of the girl in the "Biglow Papers," and Derrick's face was full of such bliss as one seldom sees.

He had always had to wait for his good things, but in the end they came to him. However, you may depend upon it he didn't say much. That was never his way. He only gripped my hand, and with his eyes all aglow with happiness, exclaimed, "Congratulate me, old fellow!"

THE END.

www.ingramcontent.com/pod-product-compliance
Lightning Source LLC
Chambersburg PA
CBHW021129020726
47500CB00003B/997